"Bo...kiss me

His conscience, a
banished to the fa
begged him to stop. To remember who
Carly was.

Yet he couldn't seem to yield to common sense. Not yet. Not until he'd tasted her just this one time. But it had been Carly who came to her senses first, who'd placed her hands on his chest and pushed away slowly.

Her breath was ragged. "I wish we were anywhere but here."

So did Bo. His bed at home would have been nice. But he couldn't deal with the reality of what they'd done, the step they'd taken that would change their friendship forever.

Friends didn't kiss each other like that...

The Perfect Wife
JUDY DUARTE

MILLS & BOON®

Special
Edition

First published in Great Britain 2007
Harlequin Mills & Boon Limited,
Eton House, 18-24 Paradise Road, Richmond, Surrey TW9 1SR

© Harlequin Books S.A. 2006

Special thanks and acknowledgement are given to Judy Duarte for her contribution to the TALK OF THE NEIGHBOURHOOD mini-series.

ISBN: 978 0 263 85642 2

23-0807

Printed and bound in Spain
by Litografia Rosés S.A., Barcelona

To my husband, Sal,
who encourages me to chase my dreams.
I love you, honey.

Don't miss our new bonus
Special Moments section at the end
of the story, where we have horoscopes,
author information, a sneak peek at a story
that's in the pipeline and puzzles for you to do!

Chapter One

When the doorbell rang, Carly Alderson was sitting cross-legged on the Italian leather recliner in the den, watching a made-for-TV movie about star-crossed lovers, sniffling back tears and popping the remains of a lemon-filled doughnut into her mouth.

As the elegant gong resonated through the custom-built, plantation-style home her neighbors referred to as the McMansion, she froze in midchew.

Oh, God. Make them go away.

She was *so* not up for visitors. Not today, and especially not now.

Half of her wanted to ignore the interruption, reach back into the Tasty Dream Donut sack for the last chocolate éclair, sink into the cushions and fall back into a fictional sorrow, rather than think about her own.

But the rest of her, which unfortunately included the eight-and-a-half pounds she'd put on since her divorce had been finalized, hoped it was Greg coming home to tell her he was having second thoughts. That he'd made a big mistake—a *huge* one—and that he couldn't live without her.

News like that would be the first step in righting her world—the one Greg had sent spinning off its axis when he'd told her he didn't love her anymore and that after seven years of marriage he wanted a divorce.

In a fit of bravado, Carly had thrown him out of the house, then had all the locks changed. That bold move, as well as taking back her maiden name, had been Carly's way of letting Greg know what a divorce meant. That things were final. Kaput. Finished.

Of course, she'd only meant it as a bit of shock therapy, a way for him to see reason.

But so far, nothing had worked.

The gong sounded again, and nervous panic sent her heart rate thumping to beat the band.

What if it *was* Greg?

Needless to say, the desperate I-need-to-save-my-marriage part won out.

She stood, and when she glanced at the telltale bag in her hands, her breath caught.

Oh, God. She couldn't let him find her pigging out. So she quickly shoved the incriminating sack, complete with the remaining chocolate éclair, under the chair cushion, a trick she hadn't pulled in years.

Then she rushed into the guest bathroom that was right off the den to make sure she didn't have any glaze or lemony goo smeared across her face. But as she looked into the mirror, she nearly collapsed in a frumpy heap on the hardwood floor.

Tear tracks had done a real number on her mascara, making her look like a raccoon with red-rimmed eyes, a pitiful little creature who was a far cry from the I've-got-it-all-together woman she really was.

Greg would probably think she was still pining over him, which had been true earlier this week. And yesterday afternoon. But the culprit this time had been a sad chick flick, a real tearjerker and…

The doorbell rang again, this time sounding as though an impatient Girl Scout with an armload of cookies was repeatedly jabbing an index finger at the button. Not that Carly had ever had a run-in with a Girl Scout who wasn't sweet and adorable.

Oh, for crying out loud. All right already.

"I'm coming," she hollered, as she turned on the water in the bathroom sink.

She half hoped whoever it was would get tired of waiting and just go away. But she'd neglected to pull her car into the garage after a grocery run this morning, so most people would suspect she was at home and in a back part of the house.

If she found a salesman—the pesky adult variety—at

the door, she'd probably practice some of those fancy kickboxing moves and see if they really worked.

Of course, if it was Greg, she'd die of embarrassment. He'd never seen her looking so wretched and pitiful.

There'd been a time in her life when she'd always looked that way, felt that way. But a lot had changed since she'd grown up, left home and gone to college. She'd gotten her act together and gained some self-control.

Yet if truth be told, she'd allowed herself to fall back into a few old habits lately, something she'd have to put a stop to before the extra weight made her feel as ugly and as worthless as she'd felt as a child.

In spite of her ability to shove the ego-shattering memories to the back of her mind, where they belonged, the words of her father crept back to haunt her. To whittle away at the perfect life she'd created for herself.

Damn it, Carly. Are you eating again? You're going to be as fat as your mother if you're not careful.

For cripes sake, girl. Can't you get a rearview mirror? If you ever need to haul ass, you'll have to make two trips.

"Stop it," she snapped to the chubby child within who refused to grow up and move on.

She reached for an embroidered linen hand towel, then rubbed at the smeared mascara.

A fist bam-bam-bammed on the door, something she might not have heard in any other part of the house, and a muffled voice yelled, "Open up, Carly. We know you're in there."

Okay. It wasn't Greg.

She nearly slunk back to the den, ready to ignore her guests. But she'd recognized the voice of Molly Jackson, who had a key to the house.

It wasn't as though the two of them were best friends. After all, Carly didn't let people get that close. But when she'd been handed two sets of keys, it had seemed like a good idea to give a spare to a neighbor in case of emergency.

And Molly, who lived right next door, seemed like a logical choice.

"I can let myself in," Molly reminded her. "Come on, Carly. Open up. We've been worried about you."

The fact that someone in the neighborhood cared was a bit uplifting.

Carly took a deep breath, then strode to the entry and opened the door, finding Molly and another neighbor, Rebecca Peters, on the porch. Stepping aside and allowing the women into the marble-tiled foyer, she caught the whiff of tropical-scented sunblock as they entered.

Rebecca, an attractive woman in her late twenties with brown hair and blue eyes, was, as usual, fashionably dressed—even wearing a swimsuit cover-up. "We came to take you to the community pool."

"Are you kidding?" Carly, who normally didn't even head downstairs for breakfast unless she was impeccably groomed, glanced at the front of the man's blue T-shirt she wore, one of Greg's that had been in the dryer when she'd demanded he pack his things and get out. "I can't go anywhere like this."

"You look fine for what we've got in mind," Rebecca said.

"That's right," Molly, who sported a white sundress, added. "You've been licking your wounds long enough, and we're taking you with us."

Oh, no. Carly wasn't going out in public. Besides, why should she join them at the community pool? She had a lovely pool of her own, complete with a stone waterfall, an outdoor fireplace, a hot tub, lush green plants and a colorful garden. "If you want to lie in the sun or swim, come on inside. We can spend the afternoon in my backyard."

"Not today. You've been holed up inside the McMansion for too long, and it's time to get out into the world again." Molly, whose long brown, curly hair was swept up in a stylish clip, pointed to the circular stairway. "Go get a towel and a swimsuit and come with us."

"I'm not holed up in here," Carly lied.

Rebecca, her blue eyes sparkling with determination, crossed her arms. "There's life after divorce, Carly. And the sooner you accept that the better."

"I accept it." But what she really had trouble accepting was the fact that a month ago, Greg had started dating. And to make matters worse, he was seeing Megan Schumacher, a woman from the neighborhood Carly had once considered a friend.

It still stung, still hurt.

And it was so very hard to understand.

Carly had worked her butt off, trying to make Greg proud of her, trying to be the perfect wife in every way.

And Megan, a full-figured woman who could stand to lose twenty pounds, wasn't all that pretty.

So what did Greg see in her?

The small voice asked, *Better yet, what does Megan have that you don't?*

For a moment, Carly faltered, her pride taking a direct hit. But she refused to believe there was something in her that might be lacking. Not when she'd tried so hard to be everything a wife should be.

Maybe her handsome, hardworking, successful ex-husband was going through a midlife crisis, assuming men did that when they turned thirty. Of course, she'd always thought something like that happened a decade or two later in a man's life, but nothing else explained what had made Greg decide he wanted out of the marriage. Not when Carly had worked so hard to stay in shape, to make him proud of her. To be the perfect wife, the kind of woman he deserved.

Why, even Greg's snobby mother, Vanessa, who'd been impossible to please, had begun to accept Carly—sort of. She'd come to Carly's defense after they'd separated, and tried to convince Greg to go home, to make things work.

But he hadn't wanted to.

"We're not leaving without you," Rebecca said as she placed her hands on Carly's shoulders, then turned her around, pushing her gently but firmly toward the stairs. "Go get your suit and a towel. We'll wait."

Carly would rather finish off that chocolate éclair, even if it was now smooshed by the cushion of the recliner, but she reluctantly did as her neighbors suggested. She wasn't entirely sure why, though. Maybe because they were right. She *had* been hiding, licking her wounds. And it was time she got back on track.

She had a lot going for her. A nice house, a generous divorce settlement. A body that, after she starved herself for a couple of weeks and worked out like a fiend, would soon be back in shape.

God forbid she keep oinking out on Tasty Dream Donuts. She'd be as big as her mother in no time at all.

A twinge of guilt reared its head.

Carly hadn't meant that in a bad way. She loved her mom and missed her, but the weight the middle-aged woman had been carrying for the past twenty-five years wasn't healthy and could lead to heart disease or a stroke. It had also kept her housebound.

Years ago, Carly, her sister and their mom had been close, clinging to each other through difficult times. But they'd all developed eating disorders, although Carly had overcome hers.

Oh yeah? that pesky, small voice asked. *What about that smooshed éclair resting in the paper bag under the cushion of the recliner?*

Okay. So maybe she might not have kicked hers completely. But with Greg gone, she'd rebelled from her rigid daily workouts and those brutal carb and fat restrictions. And to be honest, she was enjoying the temporary break. Maybe a bit too much.

But she'd get back on track.

As Carly climbed the circular stairway to her bedroom, she made a mental note to call her mother again this evening. It had been a week, and Carly wanted to check on her, maybe find out if the new diet program, a special study her doctor had encouraged her to take part in, was still working.

Her mother's obesity was slowly killing her, the doctor had told her during her last visit. Her knees were giving out on her, her cholesterol and triglycerides were dangerously high.

But that was something only her mom could do something about.

Carly had, of course, gone to great lengths not to let history repeat itself. And she wasn't about to let her eating habits get out of control.

But she wouldn't put on a swimsuit without a cover-up, either. Not with the tummy pooch she'd developed over the past month. It had been a long time since she'd been anything but toned and lean. And the thought of having anyone see her imperfections was enough to make her sick.

Not in a binge and purge sort of way. That had been her sister's routine.

But Carly's divorce had blindsided her, hitting her hard, pulling the proverbial rug out from under her.

Greg and their marriage had been her whole life, but it was time to right her world and restore her battered self-esteem.

Besides, who would see her at the community pool?

Bo Conway glanced up from his work on the bath-house at the pool as three women strolled through the wrought-iron gate and chose a couple of lounge chairs just a few feet away from where he'd set up his tools. He nearly shrugged them off, along with the other sun-bathers and swimmers, until he recognized a sweet, sexy Texas drawl and recognized the stunning blonde with blue eyes and a dynamite smile.

Carly Banning—or rather, Alderson now—was a beautiful woman who worked hard at her appearance.

Too hard, if you asked him.

She even had a state-of-the-art gym built in the basement of the McMansion, which had cost her ex-husband, Greg Banning, a pretty penny. But unlike a lot of wealthy housewives with too much time and money on her hands, she actually used her gym.

Bo had done a lot of work at the Bannings' place, a major renovation that had been the talk of the town, so he had some insight regarding the recently divorced couple that their neighbors didn't have.

In fact, Bo was one of the few people who hadn't been surprised to hear of the breakup. Not that he'd heard them fight. But he'd felt the tension between them and sensed the loneliness that permeated the walls of the

McMansion, even when Greg and Carly had been in the same room.

Still, that didn't mean he didn't like them both. Or that he wasn't sorry to hear of the divorce. Marital commitments were meant to last. And that was something Bo had strong feelings about—enough that he often observed couples, watched the way they treated each other, the way they showed affection. It had been something his uncle Roy had told him during one of their many discussions about life, love and the pursuit of happiness.

"A guy can learn a lot by just opening up his eyes and ears," Roy had said.

So Bo made a habit of people watching, couple watching. And he'd decided Roy had been right.

A few months ago, while working at the McMansion, a house that was entirely too big and gaudy as far as Bo was concerned, he'd come upon a teary-eyed Carly—or Mrs. B., as he'd called her then—sitting in an easy chair with a glass of milk and a bag of Oreo cookies.

"My drug of choice," she'd said.

For a woman who was damn near perfect and who worked out like crazy, it seemed counterproductive to be wolfing down a jillion calories.

He'd also been taken aback by the vulnerability in her gaze, by the waif who seemed to peer out at him from eyes glistening with raw emotion.

Originally, Bo had pegged Carly as being self-centered. But she'd always treated him kindly and never patronized him as some of his clients did. And soon his heart had gone out to her—as it was doing again today.

A couple of times, out of the corner of his eye, he caught her glancing his way, yet not in the form of a come-on. They'd kind of…well, he didn't know exactly. Connected, he supposed.

Her husband had a business to run, so she'd spent a lot of time overseeing both the construction and the remodel of the McMansion. But not in a bothersome way. She'd been truly interested, involved. And she'd also listened to reason when he had to tell her one or another of her ideas wouldn't work.

There was something else that had tugged at his heart, played on his sympathy.

When she was deep in thought or stressed, she had a habit of gnawing on her bottom lip in a way that made her porcelain outside peel away, revealing a flesh-and-blood woman inside.

Still, he'd minded his own business, knowing better than to stick his nose where it didn't belong.

Besides, he had a dream to chase, a future to secure.

Yet at this particular moment he couldn't help eavesdropping on the women's conversation, words not meant for his ears.

"I think it's time we go out to dinner and open a bottle of champagne," the attractive brunette told Carly. "We need to celebrate your freedom and christen your new life."

His former client didn't look too happy with that suggestion.

"All you need to do is find another man," the other woman added. "You'll be back on track before you know it."

"That's a lot easier said than done." Carly, who wore a large blue T-shirt that masked a shapely body, covered a lounge chair with a bright yellow-and-red-striped beach towel. "I've been married so long that I wouldn't even know what to do on a date."

"It's like riding a bike," the brunette said, taking a sip of her bottled water. "It'll all come back to you. And you'll realize there's a lot to be said about being single."

"I still *feel* married," Carly said. "And I poured so much of myself into my marriage that I'm not even sure who I am anymore."

Too bad, Bo thought, as he continued to work out of sight, but within hearing range. It was important for a person to know who she or he was, what they wanted out of life. In fact, he'd figured that out a long time ago.

He'd just purchased a piece of property where he would build a custom home for himself and the big family he hoped to someday have—all boys, if he had anything to say about it.

Of course, he'd need to find a wife first. But not just any wife.

Bo wanted a woman who would be not only his lover, but his best friend and a committed partner in life. Someone like him who would be willing to work hard and make a marriage work. A team player who would go the extra distance and wouldn't see divorce as an option.

Over the years, Bo had met plenty of women who seemed to be ready to settle down. But they usually lost interest when they found out he wasn't a suit-and-tie kind of guy, a man they could mold into someone else.

But he wasn't in any hurry. He'd find the right woman someday.

Still, he couldn't help feeling sorry for Carly. Or feeling as though he ought to reach out to her, offer a few suggestions. Give her some insight into what might have gone wrong in her marriage.

She'd have to ask, though.

And that wasn't likely. She was a beautiful woman who wouldn't be single for long.

Besides, Bo was practically a stranger and didn't hobnob with her circle.

He studied his handiwork on the extension to the bathhouse. Not bad. His work here was done for the day.

As he packed up his tools, he heard a vehicle drive up, and glanced out into the parking lot. He didn't give much thought about the car that pulled in beside his pickup. Not until Greg Banning got out with an attractive blonde, a couple of kids and another woman.

Damn. He hoped things didn't blow sky-high, because it was pretty obvious neither Carly nor Greg expected to see the other at the community pool.

A part of him wanted to give Carly a heads-up, a friendly warning. To rescue the lovely damsel in distress.

But who was he to interfere?

It was best if he got his crap together and headed out to the parking lot before things got…ugly.

"Hey," Rebecca said as she prepared to climb into the hot tub, removing her cover-up and revealing a new black swimsuit and the body to properly show it off. "Did you see that cute guy working on the bathhouse? I wonder who he is."

Carly looked toward the brick building and spotted Bo Conway, one of the carpenters who'd done the renovations on her house a couple of months ago, folding up a ladder.

"Actually, I know him. His name is Bo," she told them. "He's a carpenter. And a very good one."

He was also an attractive man, with a glimmer in his eyes and a single dimple that formed on one cheek when he smiled. He was rugged in an artsy sort of way. Solid, dependable, down-to-earth.

When he'd worked at the McMansion, Carly had often studied him from a distance, although she didn't think he knew she found him…interesting. Appealing.

More than once she'd wondered if he was seeing anyone or if he'd like to meet a nice, single woman. If so, she would have been happy to set something up. Yet whenever she tried to think of someone suitable, the woman fell short.

Molly, who had yet to take off the sundress that hid her bathing suit, reached into what looked like a briefcase and carried a couple of files and her reading glasses to the hot tub.

"You brought work with you to the pool?" Carly asked.

"Just some material I need to look over." Molly took a seat beside Carly on the edge of the tub and dangled her feet into the hot, bubbly water. "Your friend the carpenter is good-looking. Is he single?"

"I assume so. He doesn't wear a ring."

"A lot of construction workers don't for safety reasons." Rebecca lowered herself into the tub, grimacing slightly at the temperature. "Either way, he's sure been watching you, Carly."

"Me? Don't be ridiculous."

Bo had always treated her with the utmost respect and been very professional. There'd never been anything even the slightest bit flirty going on between them. Not even after Greg moved out and it was apparent Carly was single. And vulnerable.

But the thought that he might be looking at her caused her heart to flutter in an adolescent way.

She glanced his way, caught his gaze, then quickly turned her head.

Had he been watching her?

Nah. Couldn't be.

Yet even though there was no reason in the world why she should be so uncomfortable about making eye contact, why her heart would kick up a notch…

Oh, for Pete's sake. She tugged at the hem of her extra-large T-shirt, which hid a multitude of sins…or rather, doughnut binges. If anything, Bo probably wondered why in the heck she'd come out in public looking like this.

"You know what?" Molly asked. "I think he's interested in you. He keeps glancing your way with this…I don't know, kind of a sweet, puppy-dog look in his eyes."

"Bo?" Carly didn't have to feign her surprise.

"That's the one."

Carly shrugged off the comment. After all, Bo, a self-employed artisan, was so completely down-to-earth he didn't seem interested in the drama of suburbia. And Carly had fought long and hard to be queen of Danbury Way.

Yeah, right. Queen of an enormous mansion in New York State where her only companion was an echo of the haunting voice of a father who still pointed out her deficiencies within the cold silence.

Rebecca nodded her head toward the bathhouse. "Why don't you make the first move. Before he leaves."

"Oh, cut it out." Carly rolled her eyes. "I'd never do that."

"Why not?"

For a lot of reasons. She wasn't that bold, for one. But she offered the one that seemed the most logical. "Because I still feel married, remember?"

Before either of her friends could counter with an argument, the wrought-iron gate swung open and several children dashed inside, followed by three smiling adults.

Carly's heart pounded in her chest as she recognized Megan's sister, Angela, and her kids.

That in itself would have been enough to cause Carly to make excuses and skedaddle.

But when Greg walked through the gate, with Megan on his arm—the woman he'd chosen as her replacement—all Carly wanted to do was slip into the hot tub and drown a lobster's death.

The paunch in her belly seemed to swell and fold into Jabba the Hutt proportions. And all she could think of was getting the heck out of here. Quick.

Okay, so Greg and Megan, whose smiles had completely evaporated into the summer breeze the moment they'd spotted her, were probably uncomfortable, too. But they had each other to commiserate with. Carly was alone. And not up for any of this.

"Oh, my God, Carly. I'm really sorry about that. I never expected them to come here today."

Whether it was Rebecca or Molly commenting, Carly wasn't sure. All she knew was that she had to escape before she fell apart.

And she had to do it now.

She quickly looked at her right arm, where her wristwatch was supposed to be. "Gosh. I can't believe how late it is. I've got to go."

"I'll take you home," Molly said.

"Don't bother. Enjoy the sun." Carly forced a hollow smile. "I'd really prefer to walk. I need the exercise."

Fortunately, Greg and Megan had made their way through the gate and found a place to sit near the shallow end of the pool. So Carly quickly climbed from her seat at the edge of the hot tub, strode toward the lounge chair, slipped on her sandals, grabbed her things and shoved them into the canvas tote bag she'd brought. Then she marched out the wrought-iron gate and headed for the parking lot.

It was going to be a long and miserable walk home, but she didn't care. There was no way she'd stick around here a moment longer.

Heck, she could call a cab along the way.

But as she strode through the parking lot, just past a white Chevrolet sedan, she ran head-on into a wall of hunky flesh.

Oomph.

She gasped for air, only to catch a musky whiff of an earthy cologne.

Her eyes opened, and her gaze locked on Bo's.

"Are you okay?" he asked.

Her lips parted, but words deserted her, and she bit down on her bottom lip. As a single tear slipped down her cheek, Bo brushed it away with a work-roughened knuckle.

Then he slipped an arm around her and guided her toward his truck. "Come on. I'll give you a ride home."

Carly wasn't able to find the words to object—even if she'd wanted to. And as he led her to his truck, she felt a tad more bold and a bit less married.

Chapter Two

Bo opened the passenger seat of his dual-wheeled Chevy pickup and watched the blonde of goddess proportions place her canvas bag on the seat, then scoot inside the cab.

An oversize, blue T-shirt, the comfortable, broken-in type most guys liked for puttering around the house or garage, covered her swimsuit, yet couldn't hide a pair of long, shapely legs.

But her flip-flops…?

Nothing comfy or laid-back about them.

The white sandals added about two inches to her five-and-half-foot height. And the faux diamonds on the V-shaped strap drew his attention to pretty feet, with toenails painted cherry-red.

All in all, Carly Alderson was one head-turning package. But Bo knew better than to gawk and stare. She might think he had ulterior motives about driving her home. And that couldn't be further from the truth. No matter how empathetic he felt, he didn't get involved with classy, high-maintenance women like her.

"A wise man can't afford to," Uncle Roy had always said, before adding, "and I ain't just talkin' about money, son."

Bo climbed into the driver's seat, then started up the engine.

Under normal circumstances, he would have avoided getting even remotely involved with Carly, but in spite of his reluctance, he was a sucker when it came to tears—sincere ones, anyway.

That divorce had taken a toll on her, and seeing her ex with another woman must have been tough.

Of course, Greg Banning hadn't looked too happy about seeing Carly at the pool, either. The smile he'd worn in the parking lot had sure disappeared the moment he'd laid eyes on his ex-wife.

No telling what was going on in his mind. Embarrassment, Bo suspected. Or guilt, maybe.

Whatever it was, he'd appeared to be just as uneasy and uncomfortable as Carly had been.

Maybe Greg was regretting the divorce. After all, he'd been more than generous with the settlement and had signed the house over to her. At least, that's what

Carly had told Bo the day he'd found her with red, puffy eyes and eating a bag of Oreos.

Divorces could get nasty. Bo had seen cases where once happy couples morphed into vicious, self-centered fiends when splitting up—even when there were kids involved, sad little victims looking for love and stability.

But Bo didn't think a man would be as generous as Greg had been with Carly if he didn't still have feelings for her.

In spite of his determination to keep his mind on driving, Bo glanced her way and caught her looking at him.

She offered him a smile. "I really appreciate this."

"No problem. I'm glad I was able to give you a quick escape when you needed one."

As he backed out of the parking space and pulled onto the street, he kept his focus fixed ahead rather than on his pretty passenger.

Or her bare legs.

"I can't believe Greg showed up at the pool," she said. "And in the middle of the day. He never used to take time off from work."

Bo didn't know what to say. "He probably didn't expect to see you there, either, Carly."

"Yeah, well, my neighbors thought it would do me good to get out." She blew out a battered sigh. "And I can't believe I let them convince me to do something so stupid. Boy, there'll be a raging blizzard in August before I trek down to the public pool again—especially looking like this."

"Like what?"

She glanced at the faded blue shirt she wore, then clicked her tongue. "Like something the cat dragged in."

"Nah. You don't look that bad. My mom has a couple of cats. And you're a heck of a lot better to look at than the mangled remains they dump on her front porch."

"Thanks." A wry smile tugged at Carly's lips as she crossed her arms, arched a brow and slid him an exasperated glance. "What a charming thing to say. You certainly know how to make a woman feel good."

She was talking tongue in cheek, but his thoughts took an unexpected and unplanned sexual detour.

Bo *did* know how to make a woman feel good, but he wasn't about to go that route with Carly. She was too vulnerable. And she was also the kind of woman a simple, middle-class guy ought to avoid.

But if, even for a few moments, he could help take her mind off her troubles this afternoon, he'd consider it his good deed for the day.

So he said, "I'm not sure why you're feeling so self-conscious."

She again tugged at the top she wore, a T-shirt like several he had in his chest of drawers and refused to get rid of. "Just look at me."

He *had* been looking at her—more than was prudent for a guy who was adamant about not getting involved with a high-maintenance beauty into designer clothes, custom-made jewelry and luxury cars.

"I should have thrown this out years ago," she added.

"Clothes don't make the man *or* the woman, Carly. It's what's under them that counts." Again, his thoughts drifted to the body that shirt covered up, those legs that could wrap around a man.

Damn. That wasn't the direction he wanted his mind to go. So as a means of getting things back on track, he added, "You look *real,* as well as pretty. So what's the problem?"

"Nothing. It's just that…well, thanks for trying to make me feel better, but I'm not wearing any makeup, I haven't spent any time on my hair and I should have found something different to wear over my suit."

She didn't know him very well, and he decided to set her straight. "I'm not blowing smoke, Carly. And I *never* say anything I don't mean."

He didn't?

Carly's gaze locked on Bo's.

There was something in his eyes, something honest and solid. Something that made him more attractive, more appealing. For a moment, Carly wondered whether her friends might be right, wondered whether Bo might be interested in her in a male-female sort of way.

Or was he just being a nice guy?

He'd managed to tease her and coax a couple of smiles from her when she was such a pitiful mess, inside and out. And she hadn't found anything remotely funny in months.

The small voice suggested it had been much longer than that, but Carly wouldn't take the bait.

"I'm sorry," she admitted. "I didn't mean to sound unappreciative, but I don't feel very pretty today, and there's not much anyone can say to change my mind."

"Beauty comes from within, Carly."

She was familiar with the saying, even if she had trouble buying it. Her mom had told her something similar when she'd been a geeky adolescent, when a stupid kid at school had called her Bucky Beaver. But Carly had known getting her teeth straightened would help her feel better about herself. And she'd even approached her dad about it, knowing the family had a dental plan.

Are you nuts? he'd asked. *Insurance doesn't pay for cosmetic stuff. Besides, if you keep your mouth shut, people won't focus on your teeth.*

She'd gotten braces eventually—after she and Greg were married. And it had really bolstered her self-esteem.

So had a set of expensive white veneers.

"It's more important to be pretty on the inside," Bo added.

"You sound like a therapist."

He shrugged. "Common sense comes easy to me. And so does looking beyond a person's exterior."

Oh, great. She sure hoped he couldn't see beyond hers. There were things she'd never shared with anyone, not even with Greg. Things she didn't want people to know.

"You've got a lot going for you, Carly."

"I *did*," she corrected. "But my husband and my

marriage were my whole life. And now I'm not sure who I am anymore."

"Probably the same person you used to be, only older and wiser."

God, she hoped not. She'd left the overweight, geeky teenager with crooked teeth behind years ago.

Before the memories could draw her back in time, Bo pulled into the long drive, then circled to the front of the house and stopped.

As eager as Carly was to get inside, to slip into something more comfortable and dig through the freezer for a quart of cookie-dough ice cream she knew was hidden in a corner, she hesitated, not ready to let herself out.

"Thanks for the ride."

"Anytime."

She risked a glance across the seat, only to spot warmth in his smile, compassion in his gaze.

Or was it something else? A bond of some kind?

Over the course of the remodel, they'd spent time together, mostly just chatting. But today their conversation had taken a personal turn. More intimate.

She had no intention of voicing her thoughts, but the question slipped out anyway. "Are we becoming friends?"

He seemed to ponder the idea for a moment, then shot her a smile that went straight to her chest, causing a gentle stir, a healing touch. "I guess so."

Molly and Rebecca had suggested that Carly find another man. A lover to set her life back on course. But the only life she knew was the one she'd created with

Greg. Well, it wasn't the *only* one she knew, but it was the only one she wanted.

Yet it was nice to know another man found her...attractive. Even if she didn't feel that way.

"I've never had a female friend before," he said. "This will be a first."

Well, Carly hadn't had a lot of friends, period. Especially not men. "I guess that means a friendship between us will be kind of unique."

"Yeah." He tossed another grin her way, making the friend thing sound nice. And the male-female stuff sound...interesting. Or at least possible—*someday.*

"Thanks, Bo. And not just for the ride. For the pep talk, too."

"You're welcome."

She nodded, then let herself out of his pickup and headed for the front door.

It was, she supposed, an intriguing concept—having a male friend.

But as she stuck her key into the lock, she couldn't help thinking about all the friends who'd let her down in the past.

And the two men in her life who should have loved her unconditionally.

Her father and her husband.

That evening Bo stood before the front door of the McMansion with a grocery sack in his arms. As he lifted his hand to ring the bell, he pondered the wisdom of stopping by to see Carly, in reaching out to a woman who, no matter what they'd discussed earlier, could never really be just his friend.

But he rang the bell anyway.

And he stood there for what seemed like hours.

He was just about to turn and walk away when Carly answered.

She peered out from behind the partially opened door, pulling it to her chest, hiding behind it like a shield and looking at him as if he were that big purple dinosaur little kids watched on TV.

Okay. So she was surprised to see him. He was a bit surprised he'd come by, too. But when Carly had asked him if they were becoming friends, he'd realized how badly she needed someone who'd be honest with her, and he'd decided to step up to the plate.

Not that he expected to maintain any kind of real friendship for long, but he would give her some sage advice, maybe on how to get her husband back—if she wanted him.

Either way, Bo hoped she'd end up having better luck in a relationship next time around.

She cleared her throat. "Hey."

He shrugged, then lifted the brown grocery sack. "I thought you might need some company tonight. And something to make you feel better."

"What's that?"

He reached into the bag and whipped out a large package of Oreo cookies. "A few months back you told me this was your drug of choice." Then he pulled out a bottle of merlot. "And this is mine."

Carly laughed, a soft bubbly sound that made him glad he'd come by, after all.

"So," he said, tossing her a crooked grin and tipping his chin at the fancy doorknob she gripped. "Are you going to let me in?"

"Sure." She stepped aside, and when he entered, she closed the door and led him to the den.

As he followed, he couldn't help studying her comfortable attire, appreciating the casual way about her, the natural sway of her hips. How her pretty bare feet padded against the expensive hardwood floor.

She wore a pair of gray sweatpants that rode low on her hips, and a white, cropped T-shirt that flashed a bit of midriff. He liked that style on women, but Carly tugged at the hem of her shirt as though uncomfortable, embarrassed to show her flesh.

He couldn't understand why she'd feel awkward. She looked good this evening, even with her hair pulled up in a messy kind of ponytail. And although he'd seen her looking a lot more glamorous in the past, he preferred her like this—down-to-earth and approachable, rather than all dolled up and model-perfect.

Once inside the den, which no longer looked as though it had been on the cover of a *Better Homes and Gardens* magazine, she turned and faced him, tugging at the hem of her shirt again. "If I'd have known you were coming by—"

"Don't."

"Don't what?"

"Apologize. It's getting old."

She shot him a possum-in-the-headlights look. "What are you talking about?"

"You're far more attractive and a lot more appealing when you let your guard down."

It was true—but a real understatement.

When he'd first met her while working on the McMansion, he'd initially thought she was too caught up in herself, too wrapped up in her appearance. But tonight she looked sexy as hell—and she didn't have a clue.

Apparently, there was a lot more going on inside of her than he'd realized. More than most people realized.

He'd heard the sincerity ringing in her apologies, heard the honesty in her critical self-appraisal.

God. She had no idea. And the fact that she didn't realize she could turn a man's head, even Bo's if he'd let her, was mind-boggling.

He felt compelled to help her figure it out and he couldn't help teasing her, couldn't help the grin that pried at his lips. "So where is he?"

"Who?"

Bo let the smile he'd been holding back run its course. "You look like you've been entertaining a lover and just sent him out back to avoid being caught in the act."

Her eyes widened, as though she was taking his joke way too seriously. "I don't have a lover."

Maybe not yet. But she deserved one. And he suspected the dry spell wouldn't last long.

He set the wine on the glass-topped coffee table, next to a *TV Guide,* a crossword puzzle book, a ball-point pen, a wadded up napkin and a nearly empty glass of milk.

"The cleaning lady comes tomorrow," Carly said.

Bo hoped she wasn't going to apologize for not having things spic-and-span.

Back when he'd been working at the McMansion, the place had always been picture-perfect and more like a model home than a place where someone would want to kick back and relax.

But it looked as though she'd been spending a lot of time in this small downstairs room, rather than wandering around the big, empty house.

Heck, he couldn't blame her for that. He'd get lost in a mansion like this. Most people would.

He wondered if that's how she felt, now that she was living alone.

"The rest of the house is in good shape," she added, glancing around the den.

"If you apologize for one more thing, I'm going to start pelting you with Oreos."

She smiled in that waiflike way, and he wondered where it came from. But he knew better than to pry.

He nodded toward the merlot. "I don't suppose you have something we can open this with?"

"Sure. I'll be right back."

While she was gone, he opened the package of cookies. And when she returned, carrying a couple of glasses and a corkscrew, he offered her one.

"No thanks."

"Cutting back?"

"Cookies and wine don't go together."

He shrugged, then uncorked the bottle, poured them each a glass and handed her one.

Carly took the wine Bo offered her, and when he chose one side of the leather sofa, she sat on the other.

"So what's with your obsession with perfection?" he asked.

"Excuse me?"

He didn't reiterate, and she was glad.

Yet knowing she might be missing something left her wildly curious. "You make trying hard sound like a character flaw."

"Taken to an extreme, it can be."

"You don't understand."

"I'd like to."

She paused for the longest time, trying to figure out how to explain. She might appear vain on the outside, but that couldn't be further from the truth.

"All I wanted to do was make my husband happy he married me."

Bo didn't say anything, but he didn't have to. It had to be obvious to him and the entire neighborhood that her efforts to please Greg hadn't worked.

She thought long and hard before explaining. She

wanted to answer honestly without revealing too much. It was a tricky row to hoe, but she'd give it her best shot.

"I was brought up in a blue-collar home where we didn't have money for extras. And when Greg took me to meet his parents, I just wanted to fit in. To be accepted."

"Greg wouldn't have married you if he hadn't seen something of value in you. If you hadn't been good enough already."

There was some truth to Bo's words, but he had no idea how imperfect she'd been, how hard she'd had to struggle to prove herself.

"You don't know the Bannings," she said. Nor did he know the Aldersons. The families were complete opposites.

Bo took a sip of his merlot. "Tell me about them."

"Greg's parents? They are ultrawealthy and have high expectations for their son, for his wife."

"Did they treat you badly?"

"Not really. Gregory was all right, I suppose. But Vanessa was almost impossible to please."

"But you tried."

She nodded. "Yes, I did. And it was a constant struggle."

Her thoughts drifted back in time, to the only memories she was willing to share.

"For example, as a wedding gift, my mom and sister sent us a fancy coffeepot. But the Bannings gave us enough money to purchase a house on Danbury Way."

"You can't measure love by the cost of a gift."

"I *don't*. Believe me. My mom loves me as much or more than the Bannings love Greg, but she's on permanent disability, and it's a struggle for her to get by each month."

"I'm sorry to hear that."

So was Carly. But she did what she could to help out. "I send her money regularly, but she hates taking it from me."

"I can understand that. I've always wanted to build my folks a new home in a better part of town, but they refuse to leave the old neighborhood. Still, I'm not sure if it's because they really don't want to move, or if their pride won't let them accept my help."

"It sounds like we have something in common."

"Maybe so." He took another drink.

She followed suit, then fingered the stem of her glass. "Within two years, Greg was a rising star at his father's company and a great provider. I didn't have to work, so I had plenty of time to focus on the house and on becoming a good wife."

But a lot of good that had done.

Carly had started by working on her physical appearance—something she actually had power over. She'd even gone so far as to have a nose job, but she didn't mention it to Bo. Nor did she tell him about the grueling daily workouts with a personal trainer, the regular visits to the salon, the shopping trips that kept her wardrobe constantly updated with stylish clothes and shoes.

"I threw myself into decorating the house," she

admitted. "And as Greg gained a more prestigious position in the company, we bought the lot next door, tore up both houses and rebuilt a larger, fancier one."

Plans for a deck turned into plans for a pool, and soon they had the biggest, most impressive house in town.

All right. So Carly was the one who had pushed for the renovations, but Greg had been happy with them. At first, anyway.

"But the new construction wasn't enough," Bo said. "Was it?"

"Apparently not." She lifted her glass, took another sip of wine. "The neighbors all came to ooh and aah, but there was talk behind our backs that our house was too ostentatious for the neighborhood."

"Does it bother you that people refer to this place as the McMansion?"

"No. I guess not."

Thanks to the gourmet cooking classes she'd taken, Carly was soon known as the Martha Stewart of Danbury Way. Everyone looked forward to coming to one of her parties or get-togethers. Well, at least they used to. She hadn't issued any invitations in ages.

"It sounds as though you took great pains to be the perfect wife."

She had. "And a lot of good that did me."

"Maybe Greg would have preferred you to be yourself."

"I don't know. Maybe. He told me that marriage wasn't about how pretty I was, how perfect our house was or whether we had a baby 'on schedule.' He wanted someone who really cared about him, someone he could be himself with."

And Carly had failed him in that respect.

She'd been devastated by the rejection she'd been afraid of all along.

"My pride took a hard blow when he said he didn't love me anymore, and I threw him out of the house. Maybe if I hadn't…"

She didn't continue, but didn't suppose she had to. Bo was a man. And he probably understood where Greg had been coming from, even if Carly was still struggling with it all.

"If you hadn't, then you wouldn't be alone," Bo murmured.

"That's about the size of it."

"How many brothers and sisters do you have?" he asked.

"Just a sister. Shelby." That's about all Carly wanted to offer.

"Is she in Texas?"

Carly nodded. "How did you know?"

"Just a guess. But I figured that's where you're from because of that soft Southern drawl you have."

"Dallas, born and raised."

"You don't have to be alone, Carly. Reach out to your family."

It wasn't quite as easy as he made it sound. Her family was so far away. And besides, her mother didn't leave the house much these days. "I suppose I could fly to Texas."

"Or bring them out here."

She'd tried that once. For the engagement party.

At first she'd made excuses to put off having her family meet Greg's, which wasn't hard since they lived so far away. But when she couldn't put it off any longer, she'd prepped her mom and sister on the "right" way to behave. And then she managed to keep everyone apart until the dinner party at the Bannings'.

But even though Antoinette had been thrilled that her oldest daughter had truly "made it" and would never have to worry a day in her life, she'd found the formal dinner to be nearly overwhelming.

Yes, thanks to Carly's coaching, Antoinette and Shelby had faked their way through it all. But trying to be someone she wasn't had been entirely too stressful for Antoinette, and she'd made no secret about dreading the actual wedding.

Carly had been on pins and needles the whole time, too. She was afraid Greg and his family would learn that she was a phony and didn't belong in his circle.

That evening had passed without any serious problems or social blunders. But when it came time for the wedding, neither Antoinette nor Shelby had been able to attend.

Shelby, who'd always had one crisis or another while growing up, had gotten pregnant, which was a problem in itself, since she didn't know who the father was. But to make matters worse, she'd started spotting right before she and Antoinette were to fly out for the wedding.

They'd had a good excuse for not attending, Carly supposed. But it was still weird seeing the Bannings' family and friends fill the pews on both sides of the church.

She'd been disappointed, of course. But she'd also been relieved, knowing she wouldn't have to stress about Shelby acting up and creating a scene during the wedding.

However, Bo was right.

"I'll give my mom a call tonight," she told him.

But she wouldn't push too hard about her flying to New York. A part of Carly liked keeping her past at a healthy distance from her present.

"How about you?" she asked, wanting to get the focus off her family, her humble beginnings. "Do you have brothers and sisters?"

"Only brothers. Three of them. Pete, Jr., Rick and J.J."

"Are you close?"

"Yeah." He grinned, fondness for his family lighting up his eyes. "My folks encouraged a healthy competition among us, especially in sports. But they also fostered a strong sense of loyalty. So we might rib each other unmercifully at times, but that doesn't mean we didn't cheer each other on—not just in sports, but in school and now in the real world."

Carly found his love of family touching and decided she'd like to meet them someday, to see what kind of people had created such a nice guy.

As the two of them sipped their wine, they made small talk.

Carly was charmed by Bo's sweetness, by the sense of humor she hadn't realized he had.

Before she could offer to pour more wine, he placed his empty glass on the coffee table and stood. "I probably ought to get going."

"Oh," she said, not at all ready for him to leave yet. "All right." She followed his lead, going through the polite, thanks-for-stopping-by motions.

But it had been ages since she'd…well, since she'd felt as at ease with someone. She enjoyed Bo's company, not to mention his smile and the way her pulse fluttered whenever she caught his eye.

Gosh, maybe Molly and Rebecca had been right.

There was life after divorce.

But what if Bo didn't come back? What if she'd done something, said something, to run him off?

Her mind scampered around, searching for some reason to invite him back—an excuse that didn't sound as though she was interested in more than his friendship. After all, she wasn't entirely sure her marriage was over. But she liked Bo and looked forward to seeing him again.

She wasn't sure how to orchestrate something like that, other than come up with a bogus project she could hire him to do.

"You know," she said, creating a feasible ploy on the spot, "I've been wanting a built-in bookcase in this room. I don't suppose you have time to make one for me?"

He scanned the den, eyeing the walls, the ceiling.

"Sure, I can do it. Why don't I come by on Monday? I can measure the area and show you some wood samples."

"Sounds good," she said, feeling as though she'd scored, even if it was by default.

She led him to the front door, and as he stepped past her, his gaze snagged hers. Something—God only knew what—passed between them. Something she could almost touch.

"But it'll have to be bright and early on Monday morning," he added.

"That's not a problem."

"It isn't?" he asked. "You're not an early bird by nature."

No, she wasn't. But she hadn't been sleeping well lately and often had the coffee brewing before dawn.

"I'll be awake."

And looking forward to seeing him again.

Chapter Three

On Saturday night, Carly, Molly and Rebecca sat at a linen-draped table at Entrée, a charming bistro-style eatery that specialized in nouvelle cuisine and provided jazz in the lounge on weekend evenings.

With its warm yellow walls, dark wood trim and massive stone fireplace, Entrée provided romantic ambiance, as well as great food.

Their neighbors on Danbury Way, Ed and Marti Vincente, owned the restaurant and worked hard to make sure everything ran properly. Marti, an attractive redhead in her thirties, was the hostess and provided a friendly welcome to all who entered.

Ed, who'd been in the kitchen when Carly and her

friends arrived, stopped by the table and dropped off a basket of bread. "Hello, ladies. Marti said she'd seated you back here. Can I get you a drink?"

"We're celebrating," Rebecca told the thirtysomething owner. "Can you please bring us a bottle of your nicest champagne?"

"Certainly." Ed grinned and quickly scanned the table. "Did someone get a promotion?"

"I suppose you can call it that." Rebecca laughed. "Carly's been promoted to single and available."

Ed gave Carly a supportive smile followed by a playful wink. "Something tells me a lovely woman like you won't remain unattached very long, so I'd better hurry and get that bottle of champagne before you don't need it any longer."

When he disappeared, Carly said, "He's sweet. Marti's a lucky woman."

"I agree." Molly reached into the breadbasket, pulled out a baguette slice and dipped it into a saucer of olive oil and balsamic vinegar.

Out of habit, Carly took the basket and peered at a mouthwatering variety of oven-fresh breads. Needless to say, it was all beyond tempting, but she quickly rewrapped the linen and set the basket back on the table, opting to skip the additional calories and carbs.

"You know," she admitted, "I'm not sure why I let you talk me into celebrating. I'm not looking forward to dating. Most of the good men are already taken, and with my luck, I'll be looking for Mr. Right only to find Mr. All That's Left."

"You don't have to date the first man who asks you out," Rebecca said. "Be particular. Some women are so desperate that they jump at the chance to have a lover."

Been there, done that, Carly realized.

In high school, she'd never been popular with the boys—or the girls, either, for that matter. She'd always blamed it on being overweight and geeky.

Without the distraction of friends and extracurricular activities, she'd concentrated on her studies. And thanks to good grades, she'd received a full scholarship to North Carolina University at Chapel Hill.

When a nasty bout of intestinal flu hit the dorms during that first winter, Carly couldn't seem to kick the bug, and had lost more than twenty pounds—enough to fit into her stylish roommate's clothes. And almost immediately men began to notice her—something that made losing that last ten pounds easy.

On a whim, she'd visited a salon near campus, where she'd lightened her dishwater-blond hair and received tips on makeup application. And suddenly she found herself in a brand-new world, the Mars-Venus world of dating.

"Marry money," her mother used to tell her and Shelby. "It's just as easy to fall in love with a rich man as it is to fall for a poor one."

Carly hadn't been too sure about that.

She'd made the mistake of going out with a couple

of jerks at first, but learned to be more particular about the men she dated.

Before long, she'd met Greg at a party. The handsome, bright and personable grad student was pursuing a master's degree in business administration. And he also had a wealthy family.

Miraculously, they hit it off immediately.

Landing Greg Banning had been an incredible stroke of luck for a poor girl from Nowhere, Texas, and Carly was soon the envy of all the girls in her dorm.

But now her luck had run out.

And she was alone again.

The entire singles scene seemed to be one big crap-shoot, so she wasn't sure why Molly and Rebecca had insisted she celebrate.

"You know," Molly said, turning her attention to Rebecca, "while we're on the subject of men and dating, are you going out with anyone yet?"

"No. Not yet. I'm still settling into the neighborhood."

"Then maybe we ought to organize another block party," Molly said. "That way we can be sure you get to meet everyone."

"I'd like that." Rebecca took a sip of her water. "But just out of curiosity, what do you two know about Jack Lever?"

Jack was an attorney who lived on Danbury Way. He was also a handsome, thirtysomething widower with blond hair and brown eyes.

"He's a nice guy," Molly said. "But I think he's still grieving for his wife."

Carly agreed. "Patricia Lever died in a car accident right after their second child, a boy, was born. I'm sure losing his wife and being left with two small children has been tough on him, especially since he's with a busy firm. But he has a nanny to help."

"He's had several," Molly said. "I heard he can be pretty demanding."

"But if you're interested," Carly added, "why not take a chance?"

If Rebecca had any thoughts about the suggestion, she kept them to herself. But Carly suspected the cogs and wheels were turning.

"Speaking of giving guys a chance…" Molly's gaze scored a direct hit on Carly. "Why don't you pursue something with Bo? He'd make a nice transitional relationship."

"The whole dating thing is pretty overwhelming," Carly admitted. But she wasn't about to let on that she actually found Bo interesting—to say the least.

Rebecca reached into the breadbasket and took a slice of pumpernickel. "Maybe, if you decide to have that block party, you should invite Bo, too. There aren't that many good men out there, and he seems like a decent sort. He's also nice looking if you're into the rugged, outdoorsy type."

Before either of her friends could push the issue, Ed returned with a bottle of champagne, an ice bucket and three crystal flutes. After popping the cork, he poured a bit for Rebecca to taste.

"It's fine. Thank you."

Molly placed her hand over the top of her glass. "No, thanks. I'm having water this evening."

Ed complied, then returned to the kitchen, leaving the women alone.

"You're passing on champagne?" Rebecca asked.

Carly was going to ask the same question. Not that she was in the mood to celebrate anything, but Molly's lack of participation was odd.

"I, uh…" Molly cleared her throat, and a sheepish expression crossed her pretty face. "I'm pregnant."

Rebecca nearly choked on her bite of bread. "Are you serious? I didn't even know you were dating."

"I'm not."

Carly wasn't sure what to say, other than ask who the father was. Would it be rude of her to do so?

Of course, if Molly wasn't dating… "You don't have to answer this if you don't want to," she said. After all, she valued her own privacy and owed her friend the same respect. "But did you go to a sperm bank?"

Molly's cheeks flushed, but she apparently took Carly at her word and didn't respond.

So Carly let it drop and offered her neighbor her full support. "You're braver than I am to go it alone. But congratulations, Molly. You'll make a wonderful mother."

"A fabulous one," Rebecca added. "How far along are you?"

"About four months."

That was a long time to keep a secret like that, especially from friends. Carly leaned forward. "Why didn't you tell us sooner?"

Molly fingered the stem of her empty glass, then blessed Carly with a sympathetic gaze. "I knew how badly you'd wanted a baby. And..." She shrugged.

Carly *had* wanted a baby, but not until she realized her marriage was in trouble and she'd been desperate to do whatever she could to hold things together.

In the early years Greg had been the one to bring up the subject of children. But Carly had put him off, telling him she wasn't ready. The truth was she'd actually been afraid to get pregnant, afraid of the weight gain, the stretch marks. However, even more terrifying had been the fear of losing Greg to someone else if she became fat and frumpy. Losing him to someone who was more his class and style.

Yet Greg had left her, anyway.

Carly placed a hand on top of Molly's. "It's okay. Really. I wanted a baby, but for all the wrong reasons. I'd hoped a child would make things better between us."

But by that time, Greg was no longer interested in having a child. Or at least, he didn't want to have a baby with Carly.

She wouldn't rain on Molly's parade, though. So she gave her friend's hand a warm squeeze before releasing it. "I'm happy for you."

And she *was.* Really. But it was a struggle to smile warmly when Molly's joyful announcement reminded her how vast and sterile her house was, how empty her life.

But Carly let the subject die a dignified death.

For a woman who kept her fears and worries close to the vest, she'd opened up more with her friends during the past few months than she ever had, especially to Megan Schumacher.

Megan had listened endlessly as Carly poured out her heart about her husband, her failing marriage. And at the time, Megan, who yearned for a family, had seemed sympathetic.

Trustworthy.

But Megan was dating Greg now.

And since Carly had been burned by the woman she'd thought was a friend, she was leery about sharing too much with anyone else.

"I think it's great," Rebecca told the expectant mother. "You didn't flounder around waiting for the right man to propose marriage. Instead, you decided to have a child on your own."

"Well," Molly admitted, "to be honest, I didn't plan this pregnancy. But I *have* decided to make the best of being a single mom."

Okay. So Molly hadn't found the father at the sperm bank.

"Sometimes the best things in life aren't planned," Rebecca said. "Isn't that right, Carly?"

Carly nodded.

But sometimes the worst things were unplanned, too.

"Just think." Rebecca smiled wistfully. "In five more months you'll have a baby boy or girl to hold and love."

That, Carly supposed, would be nice for Molly.

Too bad she and Greg hadn't conceived a baby years ago—when he'd still wanted one. Having a son or daughter to fill the McMansion with love and laughter, instead of silence and emptiness, certainly would have made Carly feel better about being divorced and single.

Her thoughts drifted to Bo, to the bookshelf she'd hired him to build. The bookshelf she didn't really need and probably wouldn't use.

But at least the handsome carpenter would fill her days for a while and make her smile again.

Hopefully that would suffice until Carly could accept the fact that Greg was gone for good.

True to her word—and what was becoming habit—Carly woke early on Monday morning. But instead of rolling over, socking her pillow and grumbling about the hour and the insomnia that had been plaguing her nights, she jumped right up and headed for the shower.

The pounding spray of water felt good and refreshing, so she took her time lathering up with a new aloe-and-pear body soap she'd purchased on her last trip to the mall. Then she shampooed her hair and shaved her legs.

After drying off with a white, fluffy bath towel, she took her time in choosing an outfit.

Initially she pulled out several of her favorite slacks and tops, each one expensive, stylish and protected by a plastic dry-cleaning bag. But when she remembered Bo's comment about her looking real and more attractive when she was dressed casually, she went back to the walk-in wardrobe. Digging through scads of hangers, she finally found a pair of jeans she hadn't worn in ages, then pulled out about a dozen blouses until she spotted a simple white cotton T-shirt with a scooped neckline that ought to work.

Next she blew dry her hair in a free and easy style, letting it curl at the shoulders, rather than sweeping it up in a neat twist or chignon like she usually wore.

She was reaching for her makeup when her hand froze.

Apparently Bo liked a simple, no-fuss woman.

Well, that's what he'd see today.

Carly put on a light coat of mascara and applied a quick but neat layer of pink lipstick—minus a contrasting liner.

When she entered the kitchen, a designer master-piece that Emeril would love, she went to work mixing up a batch of zucchini muffins. As they baked, she squeezed oranges for juice, then ground fresh coffee beans and brewed a full pot.

It was, she decided, a simple continental style break-fast that Bo wouldn't be able to resist, even if he'd already eaten at home.

But she'd no more than pulled the muffins out of the oven when she began having second thoughts.

Guilty thoughts.

What in the world was she trying to do?

First she'd ordered a bookcase she didn't need. Now she was trying her best to impress a man she had no in-tention of attracting.

Before she could ponder her motives, the doorbell gonged throughout the house.

Uh-oh.

Bo wasn't sure what he'd been expecting when Carly answered, but certainly not a gorgeous girl-next-door wearing denim and a heart-stopping smile.

"You're up," was all he could manage to utter.

"You said bright and early."

That he had. But last fall, when he'd brought a crew to work on various projects at the McMansion, Greg had asked them to start as late in the day as possible. And when they'd arrived, they'd all tried to tiptoe around the place until Carly managed to wake up and exit the master bedroom, all dolled up, with every hair in place and looking like a model ready to walk down a Paris runway.

"Do you have time for coffee?" she asked.

He'd planned to get a cup along the way, between this estimate and the start of another project down on Whistler Lane.

He glanced at his wristwatch. He'd allotted an extra half hour at Carly's, since he hadn't expected her to be ready for him. And he didn't need to ask if the coffee was ready. Heck, the fresh aroma wafting through the house was enough to tempt a tea-and-crumpets man to ask for an extra-large cup. "Sure. I've got a few minutes to spare."

Carly led him through the vast interior of the house

and into the spacious kitchen, where the warm scents of sugar and spice accosted him, making him wish he'd grabbed a bite to eat on the way out of the house.

"How about a muffin with that coffee?" she asked.

"Sure. Thanks." He watched as she puttered around in a pair of tight jeans. Funny, but he'd never expected to see her in denim. She'd always come across as the linen-and-pearls type.

She'd also filled out some. In his opinion, she'd been too skinny before. But now?

Dang. She ought to wear jeans more often.

Moments later, Bo was seated on one of the pewter barstools that overlooked the kitchen work space, and Carly took the stool next to his.

She wasn't wearing much makeup today, which he found refreshing for a change. And revealing.

He hadn't noticed the light scattering of freckles on her nose before. And quite frankly, they lent a girl-next-door appeal.

Her scent, something fresh and feminine, mingled with his aftershave and the coffee-and-spice aromas that could rival any bakery on a Saturday morning.

"I didn't expect to be fed," he admitted.

She tossed him a playful smile. "Consider it a bribe so that you'll give me a better price on that bookshelf."

He chuckled. "If all my clients went to this much trouble, I'd be cutting deals and struggling to make ends meet."

They chatted for a while about a lot of inconsequential things, like the weather and how well the South Rosewood Razorbacks were doing this year.

"My family is big on Little League," he admitted, "even though my youngest brother is now in college."

"Do you have nieces and nephews who play?"

"Nope. Not yet."

Carly placed an elbow on the black Corian countertop and studied him as if he were a novelty of some kind. "Then why the interest in Little League? I'd think men like you would be into professional sports."

"Oh, I am. Baseball, football, basketball, hockey. You name it. But my great-uncle, Roy, was a Little League coach for years. In fact, when my brothers and I were younger, we all played on Roy's team."

"Did your father help?"

"He was certainly capable and would have loved to, but his job didn't allow him to take much time off, so Roy stepped up to the plate and did a great job. He was also our most enthusiastic fan."

"Having such a loving and supportive family must be nice."

"It is. Roy is my dad's uncle. And since he and his wife loved kids but couldn't have any of their own, they took my dad under their wing when he was young. And then, when my brothers and I came along, they took us on, too." Bo sipped his coffee, relishing the taste of the rich brew.

"You were lucky to have his influence."

"That's for sure. In fact, the community and the league were so impressed with Roy's ability to work with young ballplayers that he was asked to coach the South Rosewood All-stars, something he really excelled at and continued to do for years."

"Does he still coach?" she asked.

"No. I'm afraid not. When he was sixty-seven, he had a major heart attack that really slowed him down, and he had to give it all up."

"That's too bad."

"Yeah." Bo studied the coffee in his mug, then looked at Carly, saw her watching him. He knew she'd spotted his eyes glistening, but hell, he wasn't going to make excuses. It still tore him up to think of all his uncle had lost over the past few years, still twisted his gut to see how the old man's body had failed, even though he was just as sharp, just as wise.

"I'm sorry," Carly said. "For your uncle, but for you, too."

"Thanks. We're pretty tight." A grin tugged at Bo's lips. "I love that old man."

She smiled, as though connecting with him on some level.

"Roy's a tough old cuss who's full of piss and vinegar. But he nearly buckled when he lost his wife, so my folks brought him home to live with us. Just recently he moved into an intermediate care facility."

"It was nice that your parents could take care of him until it became too difficult."

"That's not how it happened," Bo said. "It wouldn't have ever become too hard for them to take care of Roy.

It wouldn't have been too tough for any of us. Roy had been like a father to my dad and a grandfather to my brothers and me. But a couple of months ago Roy found himself a place to live out the rest of his life. He handled all the paperwork himself, and the admission and move was finalized before he dropped the bomb on us."

"Wow."

"In fact, when he moved out, it was a lot harder on us than it was on him."

Carly couldn't imagine having family that close, and for a moment she wondered what would have happened if she hadn't left Texas and gone to college, if she hadn't married Greg.

Would she, her mom and Shelby have grown closer, more supportive of each other? Would they have become better equipped to handle all life had thrown at them?

Before she could consider the questions or deal with the regret and loneliness that crept into her heart, Bo glanced at his watch. "Well, that'll teach me for rambling. I'm going to have to measure that wall, or I'll be running late all day."

"We don't want that to happen. Why don't I pack up a couple of muffins and pour some extra coffee into a disposable cup?"

"That would be great. Thanks."

As she slid from the stool, her foot slipped on the metal brace she'd been resting it on, causing her to stumble.

Bo grabbed her arm. "Are you all right?"

"Yes. Just embarrassed. What a klutz." She glanced

at the barstool, wishing she could blame her misstep on faulty workmanship rather than clumsiness, then looked up at Bo.

As their gazes locked, the walls seemed to close in on them, allowing hormones and pheromones to stir, and her imagination to take an unexpected turn.

Somehow she managed to get her feet on solid ground, but she found it hard to breathe, hard to speak.

A strand of hair had slipped out of place and was tickling her brow, so she swiped it aside and tucked it behind an ear.

Even with all the money she paid her stylist for highlights and conditioning treatments, she wasn't happy with the body of her hair, with the way it never stayed put. And that's why she rarely wore it down. Loose. Casual.

Bo brushed his fingers across her brow, removing another strand of hair from her face. "You missed one."

As his touch warmed her skin, her heart skipped a beat, and she felt as though she was coming apart at the seams.

"Hey. Don't look so panicky," he said.

She couldn't see her own expression, but had no doubt he was right. There was something unsettling going on, something stirring. And she didn't know what to do about it.

"Just relax, Carly. Every hair doesn't need to be in place unless you're applying for work as a department store mannequin."

The urge for perfection wasn't what had her unbalanced, although it probably should.

"You're still pretty, but touchable now." Bo's words settled over her like a cozy, hand-knit afghan on a winter night.

A "thank you" came out, yet she tried her best to set the compliment aside, as well as the heart-pounding reaction she had to the touch of his sweet, calloused fingers, his soft, husky voice.

"I suppose we'd better get that wall measured," she said, trying to regain some balance, some control.

He checked the countertop for crumbs, then placed his napkin on the small plate and carried it along with his cup to the sink.

"Don't worry about the dishes. Just leave them on the counter. I'll clean up after you go."

"Sorry." He tossed her a rebellious grin. "I'm afraid it's a habit I've acquired after years of maternal hounding. My mom would be as mad as an old wet hen if she thought I'd forgotten my manners."

There was so much more to Bo than met the eye.

And what met the eye was pretty darn nice.

As Carly led him to the den so they could get down to business and he could give her an estimate of the bookshelf, she felt his eyes on her back.

Or at least she hoped they were.

She relished the idea of Bo watching her, especially if he liked what he saw.

Once in the den, he went to work, measuring and jotting down numbers on a yellow legal pad. Then he made a few notes to himself.

"I'll bring by some sketches for you to look at tomorrow afternoon," he told her.

"Great."

Another wave of awkwardness settled over them for a moment. Or maybe it was only Carly who felt uneasy, who regretted that he had to leave.

"Thanks for taking on this project," she said.

"No problem." He blessed her with another crooked grin that made her wonder if he might be able to work a little of his magic and skill on more than bookshelves while he was at the McMansion.

She would have loved to come up with an excuse for him to stay longer, but was totally out of ideas. So she walked him to the front door, then stood on the porch and watched as he got into the pickup and started the engine.

When he gave her a casual nod in lieu of a wave, she turned and closed the door.

She was really looking forward to his return, to getting to know him better. And there was a good reason for that.

It seemed as though she'd found an unexpected friend and confidant in the ruggedly handsome carpenter, a man who'd somehow looked beyond her appearance and found something no one else ever had.

Chapter Four

Early the next morning, while the coffee brewed, Carly went outdoors for the newspaper.

Two houses down, Sylvia Fulton was in her own front yard, retrieving a copy of the *Rosewood Daily Times* from her driveway.

As Sylvia stooped to pick up the paper, she apparently heard the sound of Carly's footsteps echoing in the post-dawn silence, and glanced up.

The silver-haired woman smiled and started down the sidewalk toward Carly. "Well, good morning."

Carly might be awake and outdoors, but she didn't normally engage in neighborly chats this early. Yet since

Sylvia was more than a neighbor, and a real sweetheart, she made an exception.

"You're up early," Sylvia said, as she approached with the newspaper tucked under her arm.

Carly didn't want to get into the whole insomnia thing, so she said, "I haven't been staying up as late as usual."

Sylvia, who was dressed in powder-blue slacks and a pastel-striped blouse, had obviously been up for a while. Her silver hair was styled neatly, her makeup applied carefully.

"Where are you off to today?" Carly asked.

"First I'll be stopping by the Rosewood Community Church, where I need to take inventory of the pantry. They keep a supply of canned goods and food on hand for anyone in need, but it's probably getting low. So I'll go to the grocery store and purchase some items for Horace and me to donate. After that I'm going to make deliveries for Meals on Wheels. And before coming home, I need to stop by Mountain View Manor and teach my yoga class."

"Just your usual daily routine, I see." Carly offered the busy woman a warm smile. "I sure hope I have half your energy when I'm your age."

Sylvia had been a community volunteer for years, and whenever anyone in the neighborhood needed anything, she was the first to offer her time, her talent or some of the wisdom and common sense she'd accrued over the past seven decades.

"Focusing on others keeps me young," Sylvia said.

"And you'd be surprised how little time it leaves me to think about my aches and pains."

That made sense.

Carly also suspected a generous spirit was what kept a perpetual smile on Sylvia's face. But either way, the elderly woman was a blessing to the entire community.

"How have you been, Carly? Horace and I don't see too much of you these days. I hope you're getting out some."

"I'm doing all right. Rebecca and Molly have been keeping me busy. Thanks."

"Divorces are difficult. My younger sister had a dickens of a time when she went through hers. But truly, she became a stronger, better person because of it."

Carly tried to conjure a smile. "I hope there'll be some benefit when it's all said and done."

"There will be. But it takes time. I'm so sorry it happened to you."

So was Carly.

Before she could comment or politely excuse herself, Horace Fulton, Sylvia's tall, slender husband, opened their front door and stepped out onto the porch wearing what appeared to be a green corduroy bathrobe and brown slippers. "Syl, where did you hide my glasses?"

"That man." Sylvia clucked her tongue and shook her head. "He's always accusing me of hiding the things he misplaces." Then she spoke to her husband of fifty-plus years. "Try looking on the nightstand, Horace. You were reading before bed last night."

Horace, who was just as sweet and as busy as his

wife, mumbled something, then returned to the house and closed the door.

"I can't believe your husband still works every day at the hardware store," Carly said. "Most men would prefer to enjoy their retirement years."

"Horace wouldn't be anywhere else. Fulton's Hardware has been in his family for three generations. It's his life. And even though he's passed a lot of the work on to our son and grandson, he thrives on being with the customers and sharing his favorite tall tales and jokes. Besides, with him away from home most of the day, I have plenty of time for my volunteer work."

"Rosewood is a better place to live, thanks to people like you and Horace."

Sylvia smiled warmly. "We're the ones who have benefited the most. We've been blessed many times over by all the people we've helped. And we sleep easier at night, knowing we're doing our part to make this a better world."

"Syl?" Horace called from the door again. "I still can't find them. You must have put them somewhere."

"I swear that man needs a keeper." Sylvia chuckled, then called back to her husband, "I'll be right there, dear."

"I'd better let you go," Carly said.

"All right. But let me know if you ever want to be a community volunteer. I've got a whole list of projects in need of helpers."

"I'll do that," Carly said, as she turned and strode toward the house.

She certainly had plenty of spare time in her day, especially since she no longer had anyone to be home for, to cook for. And if getting involved in the community would help her sleep better at night, she just might give it a try.

Because Carly desperately wanted life to be normal again.

And she was willing to do whatever it took to make that happen.

Carly hadn't known exactly what time to expect Bo, but he arrived just after noon, bringing the sketches he'd told her about.

He stood at the door in a pair of faded jeans, a chambray shirt and brown leather boots, just like any other blue-collar worker. But the snazzy leather briefcase he carried gave him a more professional air.

He smiled, and her heart fluttered to life, her senses buzzing with sexual awareness.

Truly, that's not why she'd started the ball rolling on that bookshelf. She'd only meant to share his company, to hear his voice. But there was certainly more than that going on, and she wasn't sure what to do about it.

Ignore it, she supposed. The crazy attraction was probably just a result of the loneliness that had plagued her since Greg had moved out.

Hoping to regroup, she stepped aside and led Bo into the foyer.

His presence, his voice, his musky scent made the house feel less empty. Made her feel less empty, too.

Again attraction flared.

She wasn't sure exactly what appealed to her about the rugged artisan. He was so different from Greg. And she didn't know whether that was a good thing or not. But she wouldn't dwell on it now. Not while he was here.

"Can I fix you a glass of ice tea or something?" she asked. "Or maybe get you something to eat? It's after twelve, and I know you start your days early."

"I've got my lunch in the truck. But thanks, anyway."

"Sure." She led him into the den, where they both sat down on the sofa.

He placed his briefcase on the glass-topped coffee table, popped open the lid, pulled out some drawings and handed them to her. "I'm not sure if this is what you had in mind, but I think either piece would fit nicely and provide what you're looking for."

What she'd been *looking for,* she had to admit, was his company more than anything, although a heady rush of breath-stealing sexual awareness suggested otherwise.

Still, there was an explanation for that, she realized.

It had been ages since a man had held her close, since she'd breathed in a masculine scent, melted in a lover's embrace.

Too long.

And if she really wanted to be honest with herself, the sexual drought had begun before Greg had left and had made their separation official. The emotional distance between them had started growing years ago.

Trying to shake off the sobering truth, she asked, "Which do *you* prefer?"

Bo pointed to an intricate sketch. "This one would take more time to build and be more costly, but I think it would add more to the room. It's your call, of course."

She pretended to ponder the designs, knowing she'd choose the one that would require more of Bo's time.

Good friends didn't come along that often.

A part of her—the normal, red-blooded female part—wanted more than that from him, but she did her best to ignore the arousing urge, instead opting for a friend she could trust.

Early on, while she was still a child, she'd learned to be skeptical of people professing to be friends. But Bo was different from anyone she'd ever met before. He was decent, dependable and honest. At least, he'd never given her reason to doubt that about him.

"You know," she said, dragging out the words to make her decision seem more difficult than it had been. "I think you're right." She handed him the more labor-intensive design. "This one is definitely the best choice."

"Well, that was easy." He handed her the estimate he'd prepared.

The bottom line, she decided, was a fair price. At least when it came to built-in furniture created by an artisan.

But what was the going rate for friendship these days?

No, she scolded herself. Knock it off. She just wanted some time with him. That was all. An opportunity to see whether a friendship developed.

She turned toward him, her knee inadvertently brushing against his and sending a surge of heat through her blood, warming her like an early spring thaw.

"When can you start?" she asked.

"Is Friday too soon?"

Actually, it didn't seem soon enough, but she offered him a smile that indicated her agreement. "Friday works for me."

As he placed the paperwork back into his briefcase, she stood. "Why don't you get your lunch from the truck? I'll fix myself something, too. We could eat outside on the deck, if that's okay with you."

"It's a nice day. Sure. Why not?"

Five minutes later, Carly and Bo sat at a wrought-iron patio table that overlooked the professionally designed and landscaped backyard, with its custom-made, black-bottom pool, rock waterfall and parklike grounds.

She'd fixed herself a sliced apple, rye crackers and a small scoop of cottage cheese. But she couldn't help studying the Dagwood sandwich Bo pulled out of a plastic Baggie.

It had been built on a huge French roll and was chock-full of several different types of deli meat, as well as cheese, lettuce, tomatoes, with mayo and mustard oozing from the sides....

"Are you going to be able to eat all that?" she asked, wondering how he'd get it in his mouth.

"Do you want half?" he asked. "There's plenty."

Actually? Yes. Her taste buds were urging her to give

it a try, but she couldn't afford to keep adding on pounds. "No, thanks. I was just commenting about the size."

"I've got a healthy appetite."

"Apparently." She tagged him with a playful, you're-it smile and watched as he managed a man-size bite.

After he swallowed, he studied her and the low-cal lunch she'd prepared. "That can't possibly taste good."

"It...doesn't. But it's filling."

He lifted his monstrous sandwich as if offering her a bite. "This does. And I'm more than willing to share."

"Don't tempt me," she said, realizing the man had more to offer her than a taste of his lunch.

There was something about Bo that made her want to lower her defenses, to be herself—even if she was no longer sure who Carly Alderson was anymore. She may have taken back her maiden name, but her identity was still wrapped up in Greg Banning, in the home they'd once shared.

"Mmm." Bo flashed her a grin, then turned the sandwich around and held out the untouched end. "Not even a little bite?"

She'd eaten like a bird for years. Even after cooking a gourmet meal her guests raved about, she resigned herself to small portions, tiny nibbles.

Happiness isn't a dress size, Greg had told her once.

And even though something inside her agreed, she hadn't been able to let herself go.

But Bo was different.

She could lose her head around him.

How about your heart? that rascally voice asked.

No. She wouldn't go that far. But the sandwich?

"Okay. You win." Carly pushed aside her plate.

Bo grinned, then handed her the hoagie roll loaded with goodies. But she didn't touch the side he'd first offered. Instead she bit into the part where his mouth had been.

As she savored the taste of yeasty bread, the crunch of lettuce and tomato, the smooth and creamy lather of real mayonnaise, the spicy burst of pastrami, she closed her eyes and relished the experience.

But it wasn't only the taste of Bo's sandwich that sent her senses reeling. There was also something erotic about putting her mouth where his had been, with sating their hunger together.

Limiting herself to one bite, she passed the sandwich back to him. "Thanks. If you ever tire of being a carpenter, you can work at a deli."

"I'll keep that in mind." He grinned, then nodded toward the pool, which had been designed to look like a small lake. "I've been meaning to ask. What kind of fish do you have in there?"

Fish? Was he nuts?

"It's a swimming pool, Bo. The chlorine would kill them."

"Too bad." He tore open a bag of barbecue potato chips and reached for one. "If this were my place, I'd stock that cement pond with bass and trout."

Carly couldn't help checking out his expression to see if he was truly serious, and found herself drawn to the sparkle of humor in his eyes, the dimple in his cheek. The husky tone of his voice.

Still, something told her he hadn't really been teasing.

"I suppose you'd raise deer and quail on the grounds, too."

He glanced up and grinned. "Good idea."

She could grow to appreciate that glimmer in his gaze, the boyish grin that touched her heart. "You know, I had you pegged as the rugged outdoor type."

"I am. Ever since I went on my first family camping trip."

"Are you still?"

"Yes, although I don't have much time these days. But last summer I took a group of kids from South Rosewood up to Rowan's Pond in the mountains. And I'm planning to do it again."

She reached for a rye cracker, wishing it was one of his barbecue chips instead. "Where did you find the kids?"

Bo shrugged. "I help out at the community center on Wednesday afternoons and most Saturdays."

"Why?" she asked without thinking, then caught herself. "Sorry. That was a dumb question. I imagine it's because you enjoy being around children."

There was a whole lot more going on than that, but Bo wasn't sure if Carly would understand. "I had a great childhood, but a lot of kids aren't that fortunate."

"So working at the center is your way to pay it forward."

He hadn't actually thought of it that way. "I just saw a need and wanted to help. Some of those kids are being raised in single parent homes and need a safe environment to hang out in, plus some adults they can look up to, especially during the summer when they're out of school."

She studied him for a moment as if he were wearing a Power Ranger Halloween costume on the first tee at the country club. The scrutiny didn't bother him, but he was curious about the thoughts fluttering around in that pretty head of hers.

He popped another potato chip into his mouth, and when he was finished chewing asked, "What's on your mind?"

"I don't know. I guess I didn't peg you as the kind of guy who would do something like that."

"Hey, those kids are great. And believe it or not, even at the ripe old age of thirty-three, I still enjoy playing flag football, Ultimate Frisbee or whatever. So don't knock it if you haven't tried it."

"I wasn't knocking it."

Maybe not, but he had a feeling Carly wasn't the kind to give of herself, although it might help her become a happier, more well-rounded person if she did.

Of course, she was probably the kind who'd donate cash, rather than her time.

Bo could have done that, too. But cutting a big fat check wouldn't have given him the same satisfaction as taking on a kid like Nate and getting him to respond.

"When I was in college," Carly said, "I'd thought about becoming a teacher. Or maybe even a school counselor."

"Oh, yeah?" That was surprising.

She poked a spoon at her cottage cheese, playing with it. When she glanced up and caught his eye, her wistful expression touched his heart. "But I dropped out of college in my sophomore year to marry Greg."

Bo's first thought was to say, "That's too bad." And in her case, it really was. She'd given up her goal for a guy who'd given up on her. The irony made Bo think of something Roy had told him years ago.

Everyone needs a dream, son. And if you let anyone talk you out of yours, you'll pay a mighty big price.

Roy could have been talking about Carly. Because now she didn't have a husband or a degree.

But something told Bo she didn't need to hear a lecture about that—from anyone.

"Tell me about the children you work with," she said, taking a bite of her cracker.

He shrugged. "They're neat kids. Even those with chips on their shoulders." He thought about Nate, a tough kid who was hurting big-time on the inside. "There's an eleven-year-old boy whose dad is in prison for nearly beating his mom to death. No one, not even his counselor, had been able to reach him. But…"

Bragging didn't come easy. And in this case, didn't seem right.

Who really knew what it was about Bo that had caused Nate to open up?

"But you were able to befriend him," she said, filling in the blanks.

"Yeah. I guess you could say that." But Bo suspected he'd merely been at the right place at the right time that Saturday morning.

After getting word that his mom had suffered irreparable brain damage, Nate had needed someone to confide in, someone to hold him while he cried.

Anyone else at the center would have done the same, so Bo wasn't going to make a big deal about it.

Instead he watched Carly take another Lilliputian-size spoonful of her cottage cheese. Watched the movement of her throat as she swallowed.

She had a pretty neck. The kind a man could nuzzle and kiss.

He shook off the stray thought and took a swig of iced tea from his Thermos. He didn't like having his mind stray like that. Even if he was willing to pursue something with Carly, he wouldn't risk getting involved with a woman who would reconcile with her ex-husband in a heartbeat—if given the chance.

"Well, I'd better go." He placed the empty Baggie as well as the potato chip wrapper into his lunch pail. Then he replaced the lid to his Thermos.

After he'd gathered up everything, Carly walked him to the front door to see him out.

As he stepped onto the porch, he decided to give her some sage advice, whether it made her angry or not. Whether she took it or not.

"You know, Carly, it might help you to focus on someone less fortunate. Why don't you think about volunteering some time with the kids down at the community center?"

He braced himself for a snappy retort, but saw a smile appear instead. The glimmer in those pretty blue eyes surprised him. But not as much as her words.

"Thanks. Maybe I will."

On Wednesday afternoon, when Bo arrived at the community center, he spotted a familiar white Mercedes sports car in the parking lot.

Nah. It couldn't be.

But it was.

To say that he was surprised to see Carly in this neck of the woods so soon was an understatement, but apparently his pep talk had worked.

He parked his pickup, then headed inside, where Evie Walters was manning the registration desk as usual, ready to dispense Band-Aids, warm hugs and a scold or words of encouragement when necessary.

"Hey," Bo exclaimed as he walked in. "How's it going?"

"Same old, same old," the fiftysomething blonde said. "Nate's already had three time-outs today. Maybe you can turn things around for him this afternoon."

"All right." But instead of heading to the game room, where the kids hung out after lunch, Bo first strode toward the director's office.

Sure enough, there sat Carly, dressed in a stylish, cream-colored business suit, her hair swept up in a twist.

If he were Helen Stafford, the director, he'd sweet-talk Carly into planning the annual dinner show and auction and not waste her social standing and connections by having her work with the kids.

Hey. Fund-raising was important and a good job for her. The center provided day care to low income families on a sliding scale and depended on outside donations.

Helen handed Carly some paperwork. "You'll need a TB test and to have your fingerprints taken at the police department. Then, after you complete these forms, we'll do a background check before putting you to work."

A background check?

She certainly wasn't going to need that to round up donations and plan a fund-raising dinner and auction.

Was she really planning to work with the kids? Hands-on?

About that time, Lulu Banks, an enthusiastic volunteer in her early twenties, approached and stopped alongside Bo in the doorway. "Did you want to see me, Helen?"

"Yes. This is Carly Alderson. Once her paperwork has been completed and approved, she'll be helping with the children on Mondays, Wednesdays and Fridays. Can you please give her a tour of our facility?"

"Sure." Lulu, whose hair was dyed jet-black this week and had a purple tint on the ends, grinned broadly. "It's nice to meet you, Carly. But you'll really want to wear old clothes around here. I'd hate to see you get that snazzy outfit dotted with finger paint or glue."

Leave it to Lulu, a free spirit who didn't give a hoot what others thought of her, to break in Carly.

What a contrast those two were.

"And this is Bo Conway," Helen told Carly. "He's been a real godsend, especially with some of the boys who have been…challenging. You might learn a thing or two from him, too."

"We've met." Carly flashed him a pretty smile, one Bo figured wouldn't last once she'd spent a day or two here. Something told him she wasn't prepared for kids, squabbles and dirt.

"Actually," Bo admitted, "I'm the one who suggested she apply as a volunteer. But I'm a little surprised to see she took me up on it."

"Why is that?" Carly asked.

He knew better than to say what was really on his mind, so he merely shrugged. "I didn't think you were serious. That's all."

"Well, I'd been talking to Sylvia Fulton about being a community volunteer, and working here sounds like it might be fun."

"It can be frustrating at times," Helen said. "But I think you'll find that it's also very rewarding."

"Talk about kids being frustrating, I'd better go find Nate," Bo said. "I hear he's had a rough morning."

Helen leaned back in her desk chair, the leather and springs creaking. "He's been in my office three times already."

Bo nodded, then disappeared down the hall. He was

glad Carly had taken him up on his suggestion, but some of the children could be a challenge.

And he hoped Carly would stick around long enough to see the rewards.

Chapter Five

Lulu, who reminded Carly of a young Cyndi Lauper, wore a black tank top, neon-pink shorts and green high-top tennis shoes.

"You'll like working here," Lulu said, leading the way through the South Rosewood Community Center.

"I'm sure I will." Carly's steps slowed when her guide paused.

"This is the kitchen," Lulu said, as she and Carly peered through an open doorway, where an older woman wearing a hairnet was preparing peanut-butter-stuffed celery, apple slices and fruit juice for snacks. After a quick introduction of Brenda Finn, another volunteer, Lulu led Carly to the homework room, which was empty.

"This place doesn't get much use during the summer months, but this is where we'll offer tutoring during our after-school program in the fall. Some of the kids don't have anyone to help them study at home, so we offer whatever support and encouragement we can."

"What kind of tutors do you need?" Carly asked. "Do they have to be credentialed?"

"No, they don't. We'll take whatever help we can get."

Carly wondered if that might be something she could offer. She'd always done well in school. And at times, she'd been able to explain how to solve an algebraic equation to some of her struggling classmates better than the teacher. So long division and multiplication ought to be a snap.

"Come on," Lulu said. "Before I take you to the playground, let's stop by the game room."

As she followed the campy young woman down the hall, Carly held the manila file that contained the paperwork she needed to fill out, as well as instructions about where to get a TB test. The background check had surprised her, but pleased her, too.

Kids deserved a safe environment.

She couldn't help wishing that parents—in her case, her father—would be required to meet some kind of standard before even being allowed to have children. But she shrugged it off. She'd overcome her difficult early years without any real problems.

Too bad she couldn't say the same about her sister,

Shelby, who still struggled with bulimia, something else Carly blamed on their hypercritical dad.

"This is where the kids hang out when they're indoors," Lulu said, as they stepped through the door.

The first notable thing Carly spotted—other than Bo and the group of boys congregated around him—was a colorful antidrug poster tacked to a bulletin board. The second was the display of art projects attached to strings of red yarn draped from one corner of a pale yellow wall to the other.

A pool table with stained green felt stood in the center of the room, where a couple of boys enjoyed a game of eight ball. Another group played air hockey, while two boys sitting by themselves concentrated on the pieces on a chess board.

Lulu pointed to the white, built-in shelves against the far wall. "That's where we store a variety of board games."

Near a pair of olive-green Naugahyde sofas, a couple of boys stood with Bo, chatting up a storm about a boy named Artie who'd fallen from a tree over the weekend and broken his arm in two places.

"Where are the girls?" Carly asked her guide.

"Outside on the playground. Kylie had a run-in with Nate, so we encouraged them to separate for a while."

A buzz sounded, and Lulu reached for her pager and read the lighted display. "Can you excuse me for a minute? I have to return this call."

"Sure." As Lulu left, Carly walked to the window and

scanned the playground, where a group of seven girls played in the shade of a mulberry tree.

It was nice to see them all together.

When Carly had been a child, she'd spent entirely too much time by herself, rather than risk being ostracized by one clique or another.

"Hey, Bo," a boy said.

Carly remained at the window, her eyes on the girls outside, her ears tuned to the young males behind her, and the man they appeared to like and respect.

"My dad took me to a really cool movie on Sunday," the boy continued.

"I thought you didn't ever get to see your old man," another kid responded.

"Yeah. Well, he's got a girlfriend now," the first boy said. "And she's got a couple of kids. So I think he's trying to impress her with what a good stepdad he'll make."

Another kid snorted. "He's a jackass, Ronnie."

"Hey," Bo said. "Watch your language, Nate. There's a lady in the room."

"Sorry."

Carly wanted to turn, to flash them a forgiving smile. In fact, she wanted to be drawn into their conversation, to talk about good movies, to commiserate about lousy dads. But instead, she continued to listen while pretending to study the playground and the preteen girls who'd congregated under the tree.

One of the boys whispered a bit too loudly, "Hey, Bo. Who's the hot chick?"

"She's too old for you," he responded.

"But not for you, huh, Bo?"

The kids laughed.

A smile tugged at Carly's lips, and her heart swelled in an odd, adolescent way.

"Bo's got a girlfriend!" a young, singsongy voice chanted.

"Nope," Bo said. "'Fraid not, guys. We're just friends."

Carly wasn't sure what she'd wanted him to say to a group of kids, but that didn't stop a feeling of disappointment from settling over her.

"Anyway," the first boy—Ronnie—said. "The movie we saw was really cool, Bo. And I think you'd like it."

"Oh, yeah? What's it about?"

"It's about a Little League team in this crummy neighborhood and a cranky old man who teaches them how to play ball and helps them deal with a bunch of other stuff, too."

"Sounds like my kind of movie," Bo said. "I'd like to see it."

Carly supposed he'd make of point of it, especially since the boy's movie synopsis reminded her of Bo's uncle and the youngsters he'd coached.

Unable to help herself, she turned. She meant to introduce herself to the boys, but instead her gaze settled on Bo.

He shot her a crooked grin, then shrugged.

There it went again, the warm rush in her veins, the flutter in her heart as if a swarm of butterflies filled her chest.

Whoa. Backpedal. Quick.

She broke eye contact and focused her attention on the boys. "I haven't seen a movie in ages, but that sounds like one I'd enjoy, too."

"It's really good," said the boy she suspected was named Ronnie. "It's called *Duggan's Dugout*. That's 'cause the coach's name is Mr. Duggan."

"Thanks for the recommendation." She strode toward the boy and reached out her hand in greeting. "I'm Carly. And I'll be helping out around here."

"Ronnie," he said, clasping her hand with his smaller one. He nodded toward his friends, starting at his left. "And this is Darren, Spencer and Nate."

"Hey," Darren said, his gaze bouncing from Bo to Carly. "Maybe you two could go see it together. You know, to save gas and all that."

The boys chuckled again, elbowing each other.

Again Carly's gaze locked on Bo's, and the moment grew more and more awkward.

"Good idea," Bo told the boy. Then he turned to Carly. "Are you free this evening?"

Shoot. These days she was free *every* evening. But she nibbled on her bottom lip, scrunched her brow and pretended to give it some thought before saying, "Sure. Tonight would work."

"Okay. Then I'll check on times and give you a call later this afternoon."

"Great."

Fortunately, before things became really awkward, Lulu returned. "Are you ready to meet the girls?"

"Absolutely."

Carly followed Lulu out of the game room, fighting the urge to turn around and steal one last glance at Bo. Common sense won out, and she managed to keep her eyes straight ahead.

A part of her might want more from Bo than friendship. But she'd have to settle for a movie.

Carly stood in the bedroom-size, cedar-lined walk-in closet, searching for something appropriate to wear.

Bo had called earlier and said *Duggan's Dugout* started at seven-thirty, so he would pick her up at seven. She'd tried to give him an out, an excuse to cancel in case the boys had pressured him. But he'd wanted to see the movie and saw no reason to go alone.

She had to keep reminding herself that this wasn't a date. But for some reason, her nerves weren't buying it, and she rifled through her wardrobe looking for something nice yet casual. Something stylish yet down-to-earth.

For a moment, she wondered what Lulu might wear.

She'd love to see the look in Bo's eyes if she came bebopping out the door in a lime-green miniskirt and red high-top tennies. Maybe a neon-orange scrunchy in her hair.

A smile teased her lips. She'd never been adventurous, but ribbing Bo might be interesting.

Oh, well. Back to the search for something to wear.

For someone who had more clothes than most women, she was certainly having trouble making a choice.

As she settled on a pair of pale pink capris and a white cotton blouse, the telephone rang. So she carried the plastic-wrapped hangers to the phone, draped them across the gold brocade bedspread and grabbed the receiver. "Hello?"

"Carly?"

Greg's voice sent her senses reeling, her heart thumping.

She cleared her throat. "Yes?"

"I…uh…wanted to apologize for not speaking to you at the pool. I meant to, but then you took off so quickly."

"That's okay."

It hadn't been, of course. But what else could she say? That she'd been mortified to see him with Megan? That she was hurt that he'd been able to take time off from work for the new woman in his life when he'd never done so with her?

"How are you?" he asked.

"I'm okay."

That's okay. I'm okay. Maybe on one of her next shopping trips she ought to purchase a thesaurus to keep handy for stilted conversations like this.

"I'm glad."

Was he?

Silence filled the telephone line, but she'd be darned if she knew what to say.

"I don't want things to be awkward between us, Carly."

Neither did she. But maybe he shouldn't have started

dating so soon. Or better yet, maybe he shouldn't have pursued a woman Carly had thought was her friend, a graphic designer Carly had actually gone to bat for and suggested Greg use on various projects for Banning's, the family owned and operated chain of upscale department stores.

The silence returned, and quite frankly, she didn't have time to dawdle. Nor did she need the additional stress.

"Listen, Greg. I've got company coming soon, and I need to get ready." Carly knew the movie thing with Bo wasn't exactly a date. But she couldn't help wanting her ex to think that it was. "In fact, I hear his car. I really need to go."

"Sure," Greg said. "Have fun."

"Oh, I intend to."

When the line disconnected, Carly plopped down on the bed. Okay, so she'd stretched the truth.

But turnabout was fair play.

What was so bad about wanting Greg to think she'd found a replacement for him, too?

Not that Bo was a replacement. He was just a friend. A man who made her smile. A guy with whom she could let down her guard—at least a little.

No, she didn't have a date with Bo. But for some reason, she really wished she did.

Thirty minutes later, as she waited for the doorbell to sound, Carly couldn't shed her nervousness.

For crying out loud, she felt like a wallflower being approached by the homecoming king.

And how weird was that? After all, Greg had phoned her—a call she'd been waiting months for.

He'd also asked how she was doing. Didn't that mean something? Didn't that suggest he still had feelings for her? That he might even be reconsidering their divorce?

But it wasn't Greg's arrival that had the nerves in her tummy twisting.

It was Bo's.

And when she opened the door and spotted the handsome carpenter standing on the porch, wearing a pair of black jeans, a white polo shirt and a charming smile, her knees nearly buckled.

This was *so* not a date.

But that didn't mean she couldn't pretend it was.

Once Bo and she arrived at the movie theater in downtown Rosewood, Carly hoped she'd shed her nervousness, her uneasiness. But things only got worse.

Was she supposed to offer to pay her own way?

We're just friends, Bo had said.

This is so not a date, she'd reminded herself more than once.

As they stood before the ticket window, Carly reached into her purse and pulled out a twenty.

When she tried to hand it to Bo, he waved it off. "Put your money away. I'll get it."

"Then I'll buy you some popcorn inside."

"Nah. Don't bother. I don't want the guys down at the

community center thinking that I took the new volunteer hottie to the movies and let her pick up the tab."

"What they don't know won't hurt them," Carly said.

"Oh, no?" Bo nodded to their left, where Nate and Darren stood, big grins on their faces.

"How did you know?" she whispered.

"I was a kid once." Bo grinned. "And blond hotties were always of major interest."

As they moved inside, he added, "But I would have picked up the movies and popcorn anyway."

"A true gentleman."

"My mom didn't have any girls, but she used to say she'd be darned if she'd alienate her future daughters-in-law by not making us boys tow the mark."

Carly laughed. "I want to meet your mother."

"You'd like her," Bo said. "Everyone does."

Once inside, he led Carly to the concession stand, where he purchased a jumbo tub of popcorn, a box of Milk Duds and two large sodas—a diet cola and a root beer.

Carly grinned. "Why do I get the idea that you didn't have a chance to eat dinner and this is to tide you over?"

"I ate at home. But filling up on junk food is required at the movies."

As they went into the half-empty theater, Bo chose two seats on the aisle about a third of the way down. "Is this all right with you?"

"It's fine."

Once they were seated, he passed out the sodas, then placed the big tub of popcorn between them.

"Want to start with the Milk Duds?" he asked.

Carly loved the chewy, chocolate-covered caramels even more than she did popcorn. But she knew better than to pig out, especially in the evening, when she didn't have time to burn the extra calories.

"Thanks," she said, "but I'll pass on the goodies."

"Too bad. You're going to miss out on the whole movie-theater experience."

She studied him for a moment. The subdued lighting couldn't hide the glimmer in his eyes, the humor in his smile.

The man could tempt a saint to chuck it all and live for the moment.

Oh, what the heck.

She reached into the tub for a handful of popcorn, not wanting to miss anything this evening.

"Atta girl." He shot her a rebellious grin. "You can maintain that militant health kick at home."

The lights dimmed, the movie began and Carly settled into her seat. Just sitting next to Bo caused contentment to seep into her. And for the first time in ages, she felt as if she belonged.

In a theater.

With a friend.

Sharing popcorn and laughs.

Elbow jabs and a whisper here and there.

So when he passed out his goodies—yes, even the candy—she couldn't help popping a couple in her mouth and relishing the experience. Temptation be damned. She'd just have to work out extra hard next week.

Duggan's Dugout was everything Ronnie had said it would be and more. And as the credits rolled, Carly was sorry to see the evening end.

This isn't a date, she'd told herself again and again.

But it sure felt like one. And if Bo invited her to another movie, she'd jump at the chance—no matter what was playing.

He stood, and she attempted to take one last sip of soda, but the lid shifted and a cool splatter of diet cola dribbled down the front of her white blouse.

Darn it.

What a mess. How embarrassing. And what a lousy way to end a nice evening.

Once they made it into the lobby, she nudged Bo's arm. "I need to use the ladies' room."

"Okay."

After quickly using the facilities, she tried to wash the ugly brown stain from her blouse, only to leave a wet and see-through spot over her bra. If they'd had those blow dryers on the wall, she might have considered manipulating her stance so she could hold her chest under the fixture to dry it. But there were only paper towels available.

Well, she certainly couldn't hang out inside the restroom any longer, so she might as well join Bo.

Maybe he wouldn't notice.

But no such luck.

He nodded toward her blouse. "What happened?"

She would have been too mortified to admit it, but the telltale wet spot was impossible to hide.

"I, uh, spilled my soda. And washing it out sort of backfired."

He tossed her a playful grin. "Happens to me all the time."

Somehow, she doubted it. But she appreciated his efforts to make her feel less klutzy, less flawed.

"You know," Bo said, as they left the theater, "that movie reminded me a lot of Uncle Roy. He's that same kind of guy—cranky and crotchety on the outside, but a marshmallow on the inside."

"It must have been nice having him in your corner."

"It was."

Carly would have given anything to have a *real* father figure as a child, a man she could look up to. A man who didn't nitpick about every little bitty thing.

God, Carly. Can't you do anything right? You're pitiful.

"Tell me about your family," Bo said, drawing her from the memories she'd tried to forget.

She was tempted to perpetuate the story she'd concocted for Greg and the Bannings, the story about the family-run restaurant that required her mother's constant attention, but decided to shrug off the question instead.

"There's not much to tell."

"Do you see them often?"

"I fly to Texas a couple of times a year." But her mom and Shelby had only been to New York once.

For the engagement party, but not the wedding, the small voice reminded her, stirring up the old disappointment, the old resentment.

Okay, so her wild-child sister hadn't planned to get pregnant at age seventeen. Or to miscarry right before Carly's wedding. But Shelby had a way of constantly creating drama and turmoil.

Your sister has turned over a new leaf, her mom had said during their last telephone conversation.

Another one? Carly had wondered. But she hadn't said anything. Heck, maybe one day Shelby *would* grow up and settle down.

Wanting to steer the conversation in another direction for her own peace of mind, as well as for Bo's benefit, she bumped his arm playfully. "Thanks for letting me tag along tonight. I had a great time. And that movie was one of the best I've seen in a while. I like when I can laugh and cry at the same time."

As they strode through the parking lot, their arms brushed again—casually, like old friends who'd grown comfortable and relaxed over the years.

Was this the kind of date a woman could expect with Bo?

Carly had a feeling it was. And for some reason, she was suddenly curious about the man, about the ladies he dated.

"When you're going out with a woman, do you take her to the movies?"

"Not really."

That hadn't been the answer she was looking for. "Where do you go? What do you do?"

"I'm not into champagne and roses, or candlelight and moonlit walks on the shore, if that's what you mean."

The closet romantic in her was disappointed.

He nudged her shoulder. "What kind of things did you used to do on a date?"

"Gosh, it's been so long. I haven't really given it a thought." Yet the movie with Bo had been sweet. Nice. Special, she supposed, in its own way.

As they drew near to his pickup, he added, "I don't usually put a whole lot of thought into where to go on a date. All I really want to do is have a nice time and enjoy the lady I'm with."

Had he had a nice time with her tonight?

Carly hoped he had.

As he unlocked the passenger door for her, he asked, "What do you like to do for fun?"

Fun?

She was at a loss.

"I don't know," she admitted, as she climbed into the truck. It had been a long time since she'd gone to anything that hadn't been a charity event or a political fund-raiser. She usually found them pleasant, but none were what she'd call *fun*.

He closed the door, walked around the vehicle and slid behind the wheel. "What kind of things did you and Greg used to do for enjoyment?"

It seemed as though she'd always been on edge with Greg, always on her best behavior.

"We did a lot of things and had some laughs, but I can't think of anything in particular." At least not in the carefree sense of the word.

"That's too bad." Bo started the engine, then backed out of the parking space.

As he pulled the vehicle onto Rosewood Boulevard, then headed toward Danbury Way, Carly focused on the headlights of oncoming cars.

"You know what?" he asked, drawing her attention and tossing her a heart-spinning smile. "It looks like someone's going to have to teach you how to kick back and have some fun, Ms. Alderson."

She had no idea what he meant, but anticipation surged through her. "I'm game, if you are."

Chapter Six

The movie night ended in a friendly sort of way. No kiss on the doorstep. No plans to meet again—other than on Friday, when Bo would begin work on the new bookshelf.

And certainly no mention of the lesson in "fun."

To say Carly had been disappointed was an understatement. But she couldn't very well chase after a man who'd only offered friendship—no matter how much she was growing to admire him or how intriguing she found him.

So on Thursday morning, she went to the clinic and had a TB test, then drove to the police department for fingerprinting. And in the afternoon, she delivered her paperwork to the community center and handed them to

Helen Stafford, who apparently was eager to get the ball rolling on the screening process and put Carly to work.

"Why don't you stop by tomorrow afternoon?" Helen asked. "You can shadow Lulu until you're officially approved."

Carly's first inclination was to tell Helen she wasn't available, since tomorrow was Friday and Bo was supposed to be at her house to start the bookshelf.

But reason won out.

All Carly needed was for him to think she hadn't been serious about working at the center. Or worse, that she'd been planning to buy some of his time.

How pitiful was that?

So she offered Helen a warm smile. "That would be great. I'm looking forward to getting started."

On the way home, Carly stopped by the market, where she spotted Sylvia Fulton in the produce section, sorting through melons. Even from behind, her short, stocky neighbor was clearly recognizable.

It would have been easy for Carly to turn her cart and head for another part of the store, but Sylvia was the one person who always had something nice to say, something positive to contribute.

Most of all, Carly appreciated Sylvia's maternal wisdom and sensibility, which were things she hadn't gotten enough of while growing up.

Not that she and her mom didn't have a good relationship. They did—as good as distance and the telephone line would allow. But since Carly hadn't yet told her mother about the divorce, she couldn't very well expect any advice or support.

Shoot. What was she supposed to have told her mom? That the perfect man, the Prince Charming Antoinette had been hoping and praying would ride up on a white steed and rescue her oldest daughter, had ridden off in the sunset because Carly hadn't been good enough?

No. She couldn't do that.

Carly's marriage to the Banning heir had offered a beacon of hope to both Antoinette and Shelby Alderson.

And so did the personal check Carly mailed her mom each month.

Before the split, Carly hadn't wanted Greg to know she was sending her mom money, so she'd lived under a cloak of guilt each time she'd written a check and dropped it into the mail.

But not because she thought her husband wouldn't approve.

Greg had always been generous. And he'd made it clear he didn't care how she spent her household allowance. But Carly had kept her monthly financial assistance a secret because she hadn't wanted him to realize how destitute her father had left them all, how difficult life was for her mom.

Of course, now that Greg was gone and Carly was living on alimony, deception wasn't a problem anymore. Not about helping out financially, anyway.

She supposed she'd have to tell her family about the divorce—one of these days.

Carly pulled her cart alongside her neighbor's. "Hi, Sylvia."

The silver-haired woman, who held a cantaloupe in her hand, turned and smiled brightly. "Why, hello there. I see you're here to hit some of the specials that just came out in today's ad. The green beans look especially nice. And so does the asparagus."

Carly never had been one to read the grocery flyers that came with the newspaper or in the mail, nor had she been one to clip out coupons. At least not regularly. She'd merely stopped by the market today because she needed some yogurt and coffee. But she *did* like fresh asparagus. "I'll be sure to pick up some. Thanks."

Sylvia grinned, then placed the melon in her cart.

"I want you to know something," Carly said. "I took your advice."

Sylvia looked a bit surprised. "You did? What advice was that?"

"I applied to work as a volunteer with children at the South Rosewood Community Center."

"Why, that's wonderful, dear. Helen Stafford is a dear friend of mine. She's just taken on the position and ought to do a fine job with it. She's a lovely woman, and I'm sure you'll enjoy working with her."

"She seems very nice," Carly admitted. "And I know I'll like working with the kids."

"Helen's done wonders for that program, as well as the community," Sylvia said. "Of course, having a husband with some pull in the city helps."

"What kind of pull?" Carly asked.

"George is a well-respected member of the planning commission."

Carly nodded as though she understood. But she'd never kept abreast of city politics, except to hostess a few dinners and fund-raisers Greg had wanted to have. He'd been the one who chose which councilmen to support, which candidate for mayor. Carly had been too wrapped up in table settings, menus, that sort of thing.

"Helen and George have more money than you can shake a stick at," Sylvia added. "And both of them could retire in a heartbeat. But they've learned that there are far more important things than trying to keep up with the Joneses. And they've made it a point to give back to the community."

"Like you and Horace do," Carly said with a smile.

Sylvia gave a humble little shrug. "We all try in our own way."

Planning to end the friendly chat and pick up the items she needed and head home, Carly glanced down at her empty cart, only to notice her hands resting on the handle. The polish on her index finger was chipped, the acrylic edge jagged.

She pulled her hand back, looked at the ugly, broken end, then curled her fingers into a fist, hiding them from sight. "Darn it. And I just had them done two days ago."

"I'm not sure why you young women go to all that trouble," Sylvia said.

In Carly's case, she used to bite her nails something awful. With acrylics, she couldn't do that anymore, and they made short, stubby, unattractive fingers look much nicer.

Unless they broke. Then they were just plain ugly.

"Real beauty is on the inside," Sylvia added.

Her neighbor might be right, but some habits were hard to break. And Carly had been striving for perfection for as long as she could remember.

In her heart, she knew that no one was perfect, and that she'd probably been brainwashed over the years into thinking she could even come close. But she continued to fall back into the familiar pattern, the endless trap of trying to please, to be something she wasn't.

It had seemed to be her only option, her only way out.

"Well," the elderly woman said, "I'd better head home. Horace wants meat loaf and baked potatoes tonight, and I've got to get them in the oven. He has indigestion and doesn't sleep well if we eat too late."

"I need to go home, too," Carly responded without thinking. Just like the automatic "fine" that slipped out when someone asked, "How are you?"

But Carly didn't have anywhere to go, anything pressing to do.

There wasn't anyone waiting at home, anyone who would sit across the table from her. That, she supposed, was what she missed most. The connection to someone, the validation that she wasn't alone in the world.

Sylvia patted Carly's hand, the one still sporting

perfect nails and resting on the cart handle. "I'll pray that things work out for you, dear."

Carly thanked her, but after they each went their own way, she couldn't help feeling a bit perplexed.

What did Sylvia mean by *things?*

Was she talking about the background check and the volunteer position at the community center?

Or had she meant Carly's life? Was she planning to pray that it all came together again?

Carly wasn't one to downplay the power of prayer, especially since she had a feeling Sylvia might have more heavenly pull than most people.

Hey. Now that was a plus. If a woman who gave so much of herself asked for something on Carly's behalf...

Asked for what? For Greg to realize he'd made a mistake and come home?

That's what Carly had been wanting for months, all that she really had to focus on.

But something niggled at her as she wheeled her cart through the produce section. And near the citrus display, amidst the neat pyramid-style rows of lemons and limes, the small voice that had been hounding her lately suggested that something *had* been missing in her life.

And whatever it was, it'd been missing long before Greg had moved out.

Bo arrived at the McMansion early on Friday morning to work on the bookshelf Carly had hired him to build.

Again, as he stood on the front porch and rang the bell, he couldn't help wondering if she'd be awake.

But when she swung open the door, he couldn't bridle his pleasant surprise.

She wore a pale green sundress this morning, only a touch of makeup and a pretty smile. Apparently, she was ready for him.

But he wasn't ready for the warm thud that slammed into his chest and threw his pulse into overdrive when her gaze met his.

A physical reaction to Carly was something that had never happened to him before. Not when she'd been married. Not when she'd been porcelain perfect and dressed to a tee.

But the real Carly, the one who nibbled at her bottom lip and whose innocent, waiflike gaze shot through to the heart of him, was having an unexpected sexually charged effect that left him unbalanced.

"Come on in," she said, opening the door and stepping aside.

As he carried in his toolbox, he was accosted by the mouthwatering aroma of fresh-perked coffee and something sweet and spicy just out of the oven. He couldn't help wondering if she'd prepared extra helpings with him in mind, as she had last time.

He wasn't especially hungry, but he hoped she'd offer him a taste.

"Can I get you a cup of coffee?" she asked. "Maybe a piece of cinnamon-oatmeal cake?"

"You're going to fatten me up," he said with a smile.

She sobered, brushed her palms against her hips in a nervous gesture, and appeared awkward. Embarrassed.

For a moment, he studied her uneasy expression, the hint of guilt in her eyes.

"That was a joke," he told her. "Of course I'd like some."

"I really shouldn't be doing so much baking," she said. "I've gained a ton of weight since…well, since I started living alone."

"How much is a ton?"

She blew out a sigh. "Eight or nine pounds."

"Perfect." He placed a hand on her shoulder and gave it a gentle squeeze. "You were too skinny before."

"Thanks." She tossed him a skeptical smile.

"You don't believe me?"

She looked at him as though she wanted to, and a knot formed in his chest.

He released her shoulder, set the toolbox on the floor, then placed his hand along her jaw. Her soft, silky veil of hair slipped across his knuckles, and his pulse kicked up its pace.

Damn, she was pretty.

As if having a mind of its own, his thumb brushed against the skin of her cheek. For a moment, a connection formed, something gentle and tenuous.

His gut suggested he either hold on tight or get the hell out of Dodge.

As it was, he was hard-pressed to do either.

He'd never met anyone with so much going for her. And he didn't mean the model-thin body, the cover-girl smile or the monstrous house.

"Carly, you haven't even begun to tap into your *real* assets."

She placed a hand over his, holding him close, cementing their connection in a way that ought to make him turn tail and run. But the moisture pooling in those baby-blue eyes was doing a real number on him.

Her thumb skimmed the knuckles of his hand as it rested on her cheek, sending his hormones reeling, his common sense scampering, his emotions running amok.

"Thanks, Bo." She slowly dropped her hand, breaking whatever connection they'd made.

Yet even though he reached for the handle of the toolbox, gripping it firmly, he felt empty, as though she'd taken something from him.

"Want me to bring you a cup of coffee in the den?" she asked. "Or would you rather have it on the back porch?"

"I'd better have it in the den," he said. "But give me time to unload my truck and haul in a few more things."

She nodded, then turned toward the kitchen.

He wasn't sure what had happened just then.

Something he'd be wise not to ponder, he suspected.

Fifteen minutes later, after Bo had set up his work area, Carly carried in a tray of coffee, juice and cake. She placed them on the coffee table.

Instead of taking the sofa, which might suggest he

wanted her to sit close to him, he chose the leather re-clining chair near the lamp. It was better that way. And easier to keep a safe distance.

The emotional pull he felt toward her had stirred up sexual yearnings, and he couldn't let things get out of hand.

As he headed toward the chair, he noticed the cushion was askew, as if something had been shoved under it.

He decided to check it out before taking a seat, although he wasn't sure why. Just a natural response, he supposed, since he and his brothers used to hide things under the cushions at home when they were kids.

It started one day when J.J., his kid brother, was about six and had gotten mad at Pete, Jr., for tattling when he'd climbed out the upstairs window. So to get back at the number one Conway son, J.J. had taken things Petey valued, like a slew of trophies and an eight-by-ten, gold-framed photograph of Pete scoring the winning touchdown that sent South Rosewood High to the league play-offs. Then he'd hid them under seat cushions throughout the living room.

As a result, the brothers often took turns chiding each other in the same way, hiding math books, car keys, TV remote controls. It had become a family joke of sorts.

So out of habit, Bo reached under the cushion before sitting, and pulled out a Tasty Dream Donut sack. "What's this doing under there?"

Carly appeared mortified, but didn't speak.

"What's the matter? Do you have a sweet tooth you're trying to hide?" He chuckled at his joke, but her pained expression was downright sobering.

He'd never seen any kids at her house. Had she actually been the one to shove the sack under the seat cushion?

"All right," she admitted. "I was eating a doughnut a couple of days ago, and someone rang the bell. It was…"

"It was nobody's business what you put in your mouth," Bo said.

"You don't understand." She pulled away, turned her back.

"I want to, Carly. Explain it to me." He placed his hands on her shoulders and slowly turned her around.

Those baby-blues filled with tears again, and spoke of innocence and vulnerability.

It damn near tore him up to see her in pain, even if he couldn't comprehend it.

"Okay," she said. "I used to be heavy. Fat. Geeky. And when I lost weight, my life began to turn around. I met Greg, got married, and everything started going right for me."

And now things had fallen apart.

"It's not the weight, Carly." But Bo knew that's what she believed.

She sniffled. "Deep inside, I realize that. But some things are hard to let go of."

He wrapped his arms around her and drew her into a warm embrace. "I know it sounds trite, but you've got to get a new mind-set, honey."

The term of endearment slipped out, and so did a slow caress of her back.

She rested her cheek against his chest, and her scent, something that reminded him of a meadow of flowers in the spring, swirled around him, stirring up dormant pheromones and jump-starting his hormones to a blood-stirring level.

But determined more than ever to be the friend she sorely needed, he forced himself to ignore the growing temptation. "Food is meant to be eaten and enjoyed, Carly."

She didn't respond, but she didn't pull away, either.

"I'm not suggesting you stuff yourself full of dough-nuts or whatever, but it's not healthy for you to binge and starve. And it's certainly not healthy to hide your appetite."

"I know that." She remained in his arms, her hair resting against his chin. "But I've been hiding a lot of things for years. And old habits are hard to break."

"I'm sure they are." His hand caressed her back again, and he continued to hold her close, offering comfort he suspected she hadn't received in a long time. "I've got quite a few old habits of my own."

She drew back, eyes searching his. "Like what?"

He shrugged. "Like keeping all my old clothes and refusing to get rid of any of them, even when they're ready for the rag drawer."

She swiped at the moisture under her eyes and sniffled. Then she crossed her arms and shot him a skep-tical smile.

"And squeezing the toothpaste from the middle of the tube."

"Wow," she said in a mocking tone. "Those sound like major flaws."

"Yeah, well, I've got bigger ones. Probably. But sometimes it takes a lover to notice." He'd meant someone else—a friend or a close relative. Not a lover. And he wasn't sure how that had slipped out.

"You know," she said—hopefully skipping over the lover part, "I've been meaning to ask. Would you like to come by for dinner on Saturday? I enjoy cooking. And I haven't had a chance to entertain in a while."

He had plans for Saturday evening, and he couldn't decide whether he was relieved or disappointed. Or whether he should invite her to join him.

"Thanks for the invitation," he said, opting to let her come up with the idea. "But there's a party at the community center that night, and I agreed to be a chaperone."

"Oh. Okay. Maybe another time."

"Sure."

"Well, then, help yourself to the coffee and cake and I'll leave you to your work," Carly said, clearly uncomfortable, although he wasn't sure why.

The secret about the doughnut she'd hidden?

The fact that she'd asked him to dinner and he'd declined?

He wasn't certain. But he didn't think addressing it would make either of them feel any better right now. At least not him.

"Thanks," he said, feeling like the coward he'd never considered himself to be. "You make great coffee."

Yet a part of him wished she'd hang around today. Maybe chat with him while he worked.

But he was afraid to let that happen. And he wasn't about to ponder why.

Carly Alderson was definitely off-limits when it came to being anything more than a friend. Besides, Bo suspected that once Greg saw beyond Carly's facade and got a glimpse of the real woman, he'd want her back in a heartbeat.

At least, Bo would, if Carly had once been his wife.

It hadn't taken Carly but a minute to decide it wasn't a good idea to hang around the house while Bo was working. She'd already revealed too much. And add to that the shameful display of tears…

Sheesh. How pitiful she must have appeared.

At home, when she'd been a child, she'd learned early on to swallow any display of sadness, any sign of weakness. Her father seemed to thrive on being a bully, and his comments only grew bolder and more hurtful when he sensed they'd made a direct hit.

So instead of hanging around the house, and even though the stores had yet to open, she'd driven to the shopping mall and joined a group of seniors who walked inside the building for daily, out-of-the-weather exercise.

And when she'd had her fill of window-shopping, and the store employees began to unlock doors, she stopped by Gourmet Gadgets, a trendy shop that sold all kinds of kitchen products and offered various cooking classes. For the next twenty minutes she perused the aisles and displays, then spent some time looking over the upcoming fall workshops.

Other than purchasing a snazzy new corkscrew, she left the mall practically empty-handed, a real first for her.

Lord knew she could have stayed home and hung out with Bo, but she didn't want him to think she had some crazy crush on him—especially if he thought she also had some sneaky obsession with doughnuts.

So with nowhere else to go, she drove to the community center, arriving early.

Before she exited the car, her cell phone rang. She didn't recognize the number.

"Hello?"

"Carly?"

Bo.

Her heart did a flip-flop and her pulse rate spiked.

She'd given him her cell number awhile ago, when he'd worked on the very first home-improvement project for her and Greg. But she hadn't expected a call today.

"Yes, it's me. Hi." She licked her lips, then glanced into the rearview mirror, a dumb habit that was totally unnecessary—not just because they were having a phone conversation, but because Bo had already seen her at her worst.

"You know," he said, sounding sheepish, "I've been thinking. I didn't actually tell you that I appreciated your offer to cook dinner for me. And I, uh, didn't want you to think I was shining you on. So if the offer is still open, I'd like a rain check."

"Oh, sure. Of course."

He didn't speak. Was he waiting for her to come up with another day and time?

Aw, heck. Her calendar was empty these days. But she certainly didn't want him to think she was lonely. Or desperate. "I don't have my date book handy, but next Saturday would probably work for me."

"I'm afraid that's out, too. I'm taking the kids on a camping trip that weekend. But I'm free on Sunday evening."

Relief settled over her. Apparently he hadn't declined her dinner invitation for any reason other than his commitment to the community center.

"I think Sunday would work for me, too," she said.

"Good. Why don't I pencil it in? If, after checking your calendar, you find it's still okay, we can confirm."

"Great. I'll talk to you when I get home."

And while she was at the center, she'd ask about the party on Saturday.

Maybe they could use another chaperone.

Chapter Seven

When Carly walked into Helen Stafford's office, it was apparent the director of the South Rosewood Community Center was happy to see her newest volunteer.

"I hope you don't mind me stopping by a little early," Carly said.

"Of course not. Lulu hasn't arrived yet, but it's nice that you're here and, hopefully, looking forward to being a part of our program."

"I am," Carly said. "By the way, I heard you're having a party here on Saturday night."

"It's our annual Summer Bash. We'll have food, games and music. It should be a lot of fun."

"Do you need any help? Maybe someone to decorate

or serve refreshments?" Carly hoped she didn't sound too eager to be included. "I could always be a chaperone. Whatever."

Helen smiled, her eyes lighting up. "Would you be overwhelmed if I jumped on your offer and said we could use you in any or all of those capacities?"

"Not a bit," Carly said. "Just let me know what you'd like me to do, where you'd like me to be and when."

"The Rotary Club is donating pizza. And we have several people who've volunteered to make cookies and punch, although having extra would be nice. We usually let the children take home leftovers. Homemade goodies are a real treat for some of their families."

"I love to bake," Carly said. "So count me in for chocolate chip cookies. When do you plan to decorate?"

"On Saturday at four o'clock. And if you'd like to hang out here until the party starts at six, we can add you to the chaperone list. We welcome added adult supervision, especially during evening activities."

Carly felt a surge of satisfaction, not just because she'd be making a useful contribution to the center, but because Bo would be able to see that…

Well, maybe he'd realize she was more than a pretty face.

Before the conversation could continue, Lulu popped her head into the office to announce her arrival.

"I'm glad you're here," Helen said. "Carly's going to tag along with you this afternoon so she can observe the program."

"Great," Lulu exclaimed.

"We're expecting Carly's official approval soon," Helen added. "But until then, we may as well provide her with some on-the-job training."

"No problem," Lulu said. "Let's go."

As they headed to the playground, Carly studied the bubbly young woman whose personality seemed to be every bit as bright, colorful and unconventional as her wardrobe.

Today Lulu wore a purple-yellow-and-blue Gypsy-style skirt, with a shimmery black top and several strands of Mardi Gras beads. She also sported silver hoop earrings, as well as several little diamond studs that decorated the rim of her upper ear.

The outfit in itself was flashy and bold, but the red high-top tennis shoes added an interesting touch.

"How often do you help out at the center?" Carly asked.

"On Monday, Wednesday and Friday afternoons for the summer semester. I'm taking classes at Valley Glen Junior College, so the rest of my week is pretty full."

Carly remembered her own days at Chapel Hill, where she'd had to study like crazy, and any kind of volunteer position would have been impossible to pull off. So she had to hand it to Lulu. "That's great. What's your major?"

"Liberal studies. I'm going to get a teaching credential." Lulu opened the door that led to the playground, allowing Carly to step outside first.

"I'd thought about becoming a teacher," Carly admitted, "back when I was in college."

"What'd you decide on instead?"

Instead?

The question slammed into her, stunning her with the truth and forcing her to remember a choice she'd made eight years ago when she and Greg had been attending Chapel Hill.

By the time she'd completed her first year and Greg had finished work on his MBA, their relationship had gotten serious. But neither of them had been ready to break up due to Greg's graduation, so they'd skirted the issue as long as they could.

Then two days before Greg was to return to New York and go to work in the family business, he'd asked Carly if she'd be interested in transferring to a university closer to Rosewood.

She'd been torn at first.

Chapel Hill was a lovely, prestigious college. And Carly, who'd kept to herself growing up and hadn't cultivated many friendships, had become close to her roommate, Taneka Harris, a bright young woman who'd grown up in Los Angeles.

Taneka was an honest, take-charge sort, and it had been impossible not to admire her. For once Carly had had a *real* friend and confidante.

But Carly also had a lover she cared about, a man who was brilliant, personable and bound for success.

She'd never met a man like Greg. And she'd been afraid he would find someone else in New York, a woman who was more of his social and financial equal. So she hadn't struggled with the decision for very long.

She'd agreed to transfer.

And when Greg asked her to marry him, she'd jumped at the chance to become Mrs. Gregory Banning and let all of her reservations fall by the wayside. She'd also let go of her plans for the future, as well as the academic scholarship, a college education.

A degree.

An identity she could claim as her own.

"I, uh…" It was hard enough to admit the truth to herself, but even more so to Lulu. "Well, after my first year, I took a break in my studies when I moved to New York."

"Hey," the young college student said, "life happens."

Yeah. And people made choices that seemed right at the time, but may have been wrong in the long run.

Carly had thought that becoming Greg's wife would provide her with everything a woman could ever want— a wonderful husband, a beautiful home. The respect of those around her.

But in actuality, she'd thrown away her own plans for the future, deciding they were expendable compared to Greg's.

And where had that gotten her in the long run?

Dang. She'd sensed it had been more than her failure as a wife and the loss of her marriage that had been haunting her. And now she was beginning to realize just what that might be.

A sense of accomplishment.

A purpose.

An identity that wasn't dependent upon her husband's.

"You know, you can always go back to college," Lulu said. "There are a lot of nontraditional students in my classes, people who've had to postpone their education for one reason or another."

Carly hadn't postponed her degree. She'd tossed the option aside. But maybe Lulu was right.

"I'll check into it," Carly said, although she wasn't sure about whether she had the focus right now. Or if she'd ever get it back.

In high school she'd been driven. But that had been her only way out of a tough family situation. A way to have a bright future and not become locked into the past or chained to the present.

"Either way," Lulu said, "it's cool that you're volunteering your time here. I figure my work at the center will look good on a résumé. But even if I couldn't use this to impress a future employer, I'd help out anyway. I love kids. Especially these little munchkins."

They walked past a few faded blue, fiberglass picnic tables and stepped onto a large patch of blacktop, where a basketball game was in progress.

A tall, lanky young man was acting as both referee and coach to a group of boys, many of whom had shed their shirts and tossed them on the sidelines. They all seemed so focused on the game that they'd yet to see the women approach.

"That's Stan out there with the kids," Lulu said. "He's another volunteer."

The twentysomething guy wore a pair of baggy blue shorts and a gray T-shirt with a St. John's University logo and Red Storm written in bold letters.

"Stan used to play college ball for a while," Lulu added, "until he blew out a knee and had to give up his dreams of playing in the NBA."

Carly could relate, even if she'd voluntarily given up hers.

When she'd told Taneka, who was a brilliant political science major and a prelaw student, Taneka had thrown her hands up in disbelief. *Are you out of your mind, girlfriend? You're trading a teaching credential for an MRS degree. What if the marriage doesn't work? Then where will you be?*

Carly had suffered a twinge of guilt, an uneasiness about making the wrong decision. But she'd been afraid to stay in North Carolina while Greg went home to New York. Afraid she'd lose him.

A loss she'd suffered anyway.

Another illuminating wave of reality washed over her as she began to think about the other things she'd given up to marry Greg.

Heck. She'd even lost touch with Taneka, who probably had not only passed the bar and joined a top-notch firm, but was likely running for a state or federal office by now.

Taneka had proved to be a good friend, one of the few she'd ever had. Carly suspected they'd been able to bond because they'd each had humble beginnings and had worked equally hard to earn and maintain academic scholarships.

If Carly would have had a friend like that in the early years, someone with a kiss-my-butt-and-watch-me-fly attitude when faced with adversity, things might have been different.

Carly might not have had to fight nineteen years of habits, an entire lifetime spent trying to please everyone but herself.

A whistle blew, its tone raspy and dying.

"Foul," Stan yelled, as he stopped the play, then offered a boy wearing a yellow shirt a free throw.

"See?" Lulu said. "This is what I like about these kids and this place. They're able to improvise."

"What do you mean?"

"The South Rosewood Center doesn't have a lot of funding and can't afford some of the things and equipment wealthier communities can, like different color jerseys, snazzy hoops and baskets. So Stan suggested something kids in his neighborhood used to do." Lulu pointed at the boys charging up and down the blacktop court, half of whom were bare-chested. "It's a game between the rags and the skins."

The kids seemed happy enough. The technique had certainly worked. But maybe Carly should purchase them jerseys.

She could even provide additional equipment, not to mention a new whistle for the referee.

As the women paused momentarily to watch the game, Carly recognized the two boys who had been at the movie theater Wednesday night.

One of them, the red-haired boy whose name was Nate, spotted her, too. He grinned as though he thought he was privy to some huge secret.

If she had any ESP talents, she would have sent him an it-wasn't-a-date vibe. But something told her he wouldn't buy it, so she shot him a smile and a little wave instead.

Nate, who played for the skins, beamed until a kid with a red shirt zipped by, dribbling the ball and drawing his attention back to the game.

"Come on," Lulu said. "I love basketball, and I've also got a thing going with that particular referee. But I'd better check on the girls."

"Where are they?" Carly asked.

"Over here." Lulu led her past a grassy area that sported a swing set, ladder bars and a slide.

They passed a sandbox where one girl, a petite brunette with her hair pulled back into a scraggly ponytail, was walking along the wood-beam perimeter.

When they reached the handball court, where eight to ten girls were waiting their chance to play, Carly's gaze returned to the child off by herself, who seemed oblivious to the others.

Carly nudged Lulu and whispered, "Who is that little one over there?"

Lulu placed a hand over her mouth and lowered her

voice. "That's Rachel Callaghan. She's new. Her father passed away a few years back, and her mother left her with a friend one evening, but apparently never came back for her."

"How sad."

"Yeah. We do get some kids coming from tough situations. And she's one of them. Nate is another." Lulu nodded toward the basketball court, where the boy knelt to tie his shoelace. His bushy auburn hair needed a trim—or at least a comb.

He was not only one of the boys who'd tailed her and Bo to the movies, but the kid who'd had three time-outs on Wednesday, the boy Bo had talked to.

There was a sadness about Nate, and Carly hoped he was having a better day. But she was especially drawn to Rachel, who didn't appear to fit in with the others.

Had they excluded her? Or had Rachel, as Carly had often done, chosen to be a loner?

"Excuse me," Carly said to Lulu. Then she strode toward the sandbox, where Rachel concentrated on placing one foot in front of the other as if she were walking on a tightrope at the circus.

"You make that look easy," Carly said. "But I'll bet it's hard."

Rachel didn't respond or look up until she reached the corner, and when she did, she squinted in the bright sunlight. "Not for me. I've been practicing."

Carly took a step to the left to block the rays from Rachel's eyes. "Would you mind if I gave it a try?"

The little girl shrugged as if to say suit yourself, but Carly spotted a flicker of curiosity. Or maybe it had merely been amusement. Either way, there'd been a brief display of interest.

As Carly stepped onto the narrow wooden beam, she realized it would have been more appropriate for her to wear jeans instead of a sundress, sneakers instead of stylish white sandals.

She'd meant to purposely sway on the beam, to make it apparent that she wasn't as capable and balanced as the child, but she stumbled anyway, her foot landing in the sand. "Oops."

"That's pretty good for your first try," Rachel said. "But if you want to be *really* good, you can't quit trying, even if you mess up."

"Thanks for the advice." Carly shot her a smile.

When the child returned a grin, something swelled in Carly's chest, providing an additional hint at what had been missing in her life, although not enough of a clue to know for sure.

"Don't look at your feet," Rachel said. "It works better if you watch where you're going, not where you are."

"Rachel is always playing on the bars and stuff," said a tall blond girl who'd wandered over to the sandbox. "She wants to be in the Olympics someday."

Apparently, Carly's interest in Rachel had spiked the curiosity of the others.

Their focus appeared to be on Carly, but hers was drawn to the child whose stained yellow top and frayed denim shorts suggested a humble homelife, one of hand-me-down clothes and fix-it-yourself meals.

"But Rachel won't get to the Olympics," another girl said. "Real gymnasts start when they're little kids and take lessons every single day. And it costs parents lots of money. I watched a special on TV about it."

Carly's heart went out to the child whose dream was ridiculed, but the little brunette stepped onto the beam and continued to balance there, to look ahead, to place one worn tennis shoe in front of the other.

Rachel was a dreamer, Carly realized. And with her spirit, she was bound to beat the odds.

"You know," Carly told all the girls, "competition and winning gold medals takes determination and hard work. And from what I've seen, Rachel has everything she needs."

"Everything but a coach and a real gym," the same pint-size naysayer added.

"Who knows?" Carly asked. "Maybe the center will provide gymnastics classes someday."

And *that,* she immediately decided, was something else she would check into. And try to provide, if she could.

The jaded preteen appeared undaunted. "That won't happen, either. The center can't even afford to hire people to work here. They gotta get people who will do things for free."

When the other girls went back to playing handball, Rachel turned to Carly. "It's dumb to listen to stuff like that."

"You mean we shouldn't listen to people who say we can't do things that we know we can?"

Rachel nodded, then started her walk all over again.

The girl had a pragmatism that went beyond sand, wooden beams and balance, beyond childhood.

Carly had never seen such an indomitable spirit or such wisdom in one so young.

Too bad Carly hadn't had a friend like Rachel when she was ten.

On Saturday morning, Carly baked six dozen chocolate chip cookies, then carefully packed them in plastic containers and placed them in her car to take to the community center.

Around three in the afternoon, she stood in the walk-in closet in her bedroom, realizing that in spite of having a vast selection of stylish and elegant clothing, she was going to need to shop for appropriate outfits to wear while working with the children.

She ended up choosing a pair of black slacks and a white blouse, then left the house and drove to the center.

As the first children began to gather in the balloon-and-crepe-paper-adorned game room, Bo walked in wearing a pair of faded blue denim jeans and a new black T-shirt.

She thought she'd been prepared to see him, but her heart still skipped a beat, her breath still caught when he entered.

He scanned the room, no doubt checking out the red-and-white crepe paper that Carly and Lulu had draped throughout the room. When his gaze met Carly's, he strode across the scarred hardwood floor.

She placed the last of the paper cups near the punch bowl and ladle, then returned his dazzling smile with one of her own.

His presence was doing a real number on her pulse rate and on her senses, and she wondered if he felt it, too. The attraction, the sexual awareness.

"Helen said they welcome chaperones at these events," she said, trying to sidestep the effect he had on her. "So, since I was free this evening…" She didn't finish the explanation.

"Well, I'm glad you came."

He was?

"It's nice to have a few adults to talk to."

She wasn't sure what she'd been expecting him to say, so she tried to shrug off disappointment over the fact that his broad smile probably had nothing to do with her in particular.

He scanned the room again. "Who did Helen finally get to decorate? She'd asked me, but I told them I couldn't get here until six."

"Lulu and I did it." Carly placed her hand on the red plastic that would protect the table from punch splatters, her fingers stroking the sleek throwaway material. "I wish we would have had some helium balloons."

He scanned the room again, nodding sagely. "You guys did a good job, considering what you had to work with."

His hair was damp, and as his head turned, she caught

the hint of a masculine shampoo and body soap, a woodsy, musky-fresh scent.

She fought the urge to close her eyes and relish another slow, lazy whiff.

"Hey," Lulu said, as she approached with tall, lanky Stan in tow. "Helen wondered if you two would patrol outdoors for the first hour, then we'll relieve you."

"Sure," Carly said, turning to Bo. "Is that all right with you?"

"Absolutely." He placed a hand on her shoulder, a possessive touch that lingered a bit longer than necessary and sent a flutter of heat through her veins. "Let's go welcome the kids as they arrive."

As Carly walked with Bo toward the doorway, his hand slid slowly to her back before he withdrew it completely, breaking the slight connection they'd had.

A connection she missed more than she dared admit.

Bo didn't have any idea why he'd touched Carly so intimately. It had just sort of happened. And just as naturally, he'd realized he needed to take his hand from her back, letting it flop to his side.

Their conversation ceased until they reached the parking lot, where they were supposed to monitor the perimeter of the building.

Down the street, Nate trudged along the sidewalk. A scowl on his freckled face bore evidence of that constant chip on his shoulder. But when he glanced up and spotted Bo, he brightened.

Or maybe it was Bo's pretty blond companion that had sparked the adolescent's attention.

Either way, Bo was glad he'd come. "Hey, Nate. You made it. I was hoping you would."

"Yeah, well, I didn't have anything else to do."

Like sitting in the kitchen and counting flowers on the wallpaper, Bo supposed. Or skipping stones across the lake at the park.

"I know what you mean," he told the boy. "I had a lot of other things I could have done, but I thought it would be more fun to come to a party."

"Then what are you doing out here?" Nate asked, skepticism in his tone.

"I'd rather be inside." Bo nodded toward the front door of the building. "But I've got to talk to any parents who might show up."

Nate looked at Carly, a wry grin forming. "Yeah, that's too bad. But it looks like you got good company."

"Yep." Bo glanced at Carly and winked. "So I can't complain."

Nate chuckled, then shoved his hands in the pockets of his faded black cargo pants. "Later, dude."

"Yeah. Later." Bo watched Nate go inside, the hems of his baggy pants brushing against the ground.

"Is he the center's top troublemaker?" Carly asked.

"He's a good kid. But he's had some tough breaks, and he acts out. I'm trying to connect with him and let him know that men like his dad are rare, and that he doesn't have to go that route."

"Are you making any headway?" she asked.

"I think so." Bo strode across the sidewalk and picked up an empty potato chip bag that littered the lawn, planning to throw it in the trash bin at the rear of the building. "You know, nobody likes to admit it—and we try hard not to show it—but we all have our favorites around here. And Nate is mine."

The next child to arrive was Rachel, who walked up the sidewalk alone, an untied shoelace flip-flopping against the concrete.

"Hi, Rachel," Carly said. "I'm so glad you came."

The girl shrugged. "It gets kind of boring at home."

Then she walked up the steps and entered the front door.

"That one's mine," Carly said.

"Excuse me?"

"My favorite."

Bo grinned. "That didn't take long."

Carly didn't respond at first. "There's just something about her. She's got such pride and determination. But she's swimming against the current."

"A lot of these kids have two strikes against them before they even step up to the plate."

"Well, my heart goes out to all of them," Carly admitted. "But there's something about Rachel that really gets to me."

"I know what you mean. That's why I volunteer to work here."

"What do you know about Rachel's homelife?" Carly asked.

"Not much. She lives with a woman who works a couple of jobs. Apparently there are several teenagers living in the house who look after her at times."

"Well, apparently, no one laid out Rachel's clothes. She's worn that same outfit two days in a row."

The soft Southern drawl that always laced Carly's voice had become more pronounced and was tinged with emotion, but before Bo could decide whether to address it or not, to admit that some of the kids had a way of doing that to him, too, a wave of children began to arrive.

They came in small groups, some on bikes, a few on skateboards, but most on foot.

When there no longer appeared to be any more kids trickling in, Bo asked Carly if she'd like to take a walk around the building, then check out the parking lot.

"Sure. What are we looking for?"

"Anyone who's supposed to be inside or any vagrants hanging around. That sort of thing."

As they walked, Carly appeared pensive, then she nudged his arm. "I talked to Helen about a gymnastics program, and she seemed to think it was out of reach for us financially at this point. And even when I suggested paying for it myself, she was concerned about insurance and liability issues. Apparently, there's some kind of clause in the lease agreement with the city that makes it a bigger problem."

"That's too bad, especially since you're willing to fund it."

"Can I ask you a question?"

"Sure."

"Do you see anything wrong with me going to Rachel's guardian and asking if she'd let me take Rachel to a gymnastics school and provide lessons for her?"

"I don't think so. I'd like to take Nate home with me someday and let him meet my dad and brothers."

"Your mom, too?" Carly asked.

"Yes, of course. But I'm more concerned about letting him have some exposure to men who respect women, men who don't resort to violence to settle disputes."

Carly nudged his arm again, and when he met her gaze, she graced him with a pretty smile. "You're a great guy, Bo."

There was something about her compliment that caused his head to swell, his ego to soar, his blood to pump. And it wasn't just the words. It was the sparkle of sincerity in her eyes, the warmth of her smile. The softness of her voice.

"Thanks. You're kind of special yourself."

They stood there for a moment, eyes locked, hearts communicating in a buzz of silence.

The wind had kicked up a bit, stirring a whiff of her springtime scent and setting off a fresh flurry of pheromones.

When a wisp of hair blew across her cheek, Bo brushed it aside.

An almost overwhelming urge to kiss her settled over him, and he'd be damned if he knew where it had come from. Or what had provoked it.

All he knew was that he wanted to brush his lips across hers, to take her in his arms and pull her close, to taste her kiss and see where it all led.

And how stupid was that?

Bo had only meant to offer Carly his friendship, not complicate their lives. And kissing the pretty young socialite would definitely complicate things.

So he tore his gaze away and resumed walking. If she'd suspected he'd been about to kiss her, she didn't let on and merely strolled beside him.

He decided to shift the conversation to something safe, to get things—and himself—back on track. "Does Greg know you're helping out at the center?"

"No."

"Do you talk to him often?" The question seemed out of line, and Bo wasn't sure why he'd asked it. Curiosity, he supposed.

It was obvious that Carly wanted the man back. And if her ex still cared for her enough to stop by or call…

"I talked to him right before you and I went to the movies," she said.

Had she told him they were going?

It hadn't been a date, but the fact that they'd gone together might have made Greg think that it was, that there might be something starting between them.

Jealousy was a funny thing. Sometimes a guy didn't appreciate what he had until it was gone.

"Greg apologized for not speaking to me at the pool," she added. "And he told me he didn't want things to be awkward between us."

Oh, yeah?

Bo had a feeling there was more to the conversation than that, and for some reason the urge to pry was killing him. But neither Greg's call nor their personal conversation was any of his business.

"That was nice of him to consider your feelings," Bo said. At least, he supposed it was nice.

Their arms brushed again, and he had the urge to both reach for her hand and to jerk his arm away at the same time.

He wasn't at all happy about being attracted to a woman he had never meant to pursue in the first place. But he wasn't sure what to do about it now. Not when he had a couple days left to work on the bookshelf in her den. Not when she was now helping out at the center and he'd be rubbing elbows with her every Wednesday afternoon.

And not when that damn sexual attraction was growing to a dangerous level.

Chapter Eight

Carly could have sworn that Bo was going to kiss her outside the community center on Saturday evening. And when he hadn't, she'd suffered a pang of disappointment, which she'd tried her best to hide for the rest of the evening.

There were times over the past two weeks when he'd sent her mixed messages, but he never crossed any invisible boundaries and always behaved like a perfect gentleman, like the friend he'd become.

As a result, her respect for him continued to grow steadily.

But so did her attraction. And she'd begun to realize she wanted more from him than friendship.

Yet there didn't seem to be anything she could do about that.

If she could be sure he felt the same way, she'd be more assertive. But she was recovering from the ultimate rejection, and setting herself up for another wasn't something she was willing to do. So for that reason, she decided to back off a bit and give Bo some space—even though keeping her distance was making her crazy.

The rest of the weekend had been uneventful, and she'd spent it at home alone, where she kept finding herself wandering into the den, studying the handiwork Bo had created and running her hand along the mahogany that he'd touched earlier.

Bright and early on Monday, when Bo was due back, she decided not to go into Martha Stewart mode and whip up any baked goodies. So she welcomed Bo into the house and offered him only coffee.

She sensed that he was a little...disappointed. Of course, that might have only been because he had a sweet tooth and had been looking forward to something more.

Heck. Maybe he wasn't sending mixed messages at all. She was probably just reading them wrong.

Still, the words nearly stuck in her throat when she told him she was going to leave him to his work, that she had errands to run.

But that's what she did.

She walked the mall with the seniors again that morning, and when Macy's opened, she picked up a couple of outfits that were suitable to wear while working with the kids.

There was a panicky moment when she realized she needed to choose a size eight in the new jeans, rather than a six. But her weight had leveled out these past two weeks, putting an end to the steady uphill climb.

Of course, a while back, when she'd mentioned the extra pounds she'd put on, Bo had placed a hand on her shoulder and given it a gentle squeeze. "That's perfect," he'd said, his eyes sincere. "You were too skinny before."

She hadn't believed him then. And she wasn't completely convinced now. But there was something nice about seeing herself the way Bo did.

Once she'd thrown her packages into the trunk of her car, she headed for the center, arriving early as usual, yet wishing she was still at home—in the den, watching Bo work.

But she certainly didn't want him to think she had nothing better to do than to fawn over him—something that would have been *way* too easy to do.

How pitiful was that?

After entering the center and greeting Evie Walters at the registration desk and Helen in her office, Carly went out to the playground, where Stan was rounding up the boys for another game of basketball. This time, a couple of girls asked to play and were assigned to the rags' team.

Carly scanned the grounds until she spotted Rachel standing near the ladder bars, and made her way to the climbing structure, where the child was studying her palm.

"What are you doing?" Carly asked.

"Just checking out my blister." Rachel looked up, a crooked smile gracing her lightly freckled face, then lifted her hand as though the red, raised spot was a badge of honor. "Cool, huh?" Her grin broadened.

"Yes, it is," Carly said. "But I'll bet it hurts."

Rachel shrugged. "Not really."

The girl was tough and, apparently, not one to complain.

Carly could relate to Rachel's drive. She'd tried hard, too—first at academics when she'd been in school, then at being the perfect wife when she'd gotten married. And she'd attained a few blisters along the way herself.

Emotional blisters.

But rather than badges of honor, Carly saw them as signs of defeat.

Rachel, on the other hand, seemed undaunted. And Carly suspected that she would weather whatever curves life threw her way. In fact, she'd probably sidestepped a few already.

Too bad Carly didn't have the same determination. The same attitude toward criticism.

Especially when it came to her own.

Once, while in college, Carly had received an eighty-two on a biology test, and she'd thought the sky had fallen.

"What're you whining about?" Taneka had asked. "Three-quarters of the class failed. It's not your fault. The professor is getting paid to get the message across, and apparently he's the one who bombed."

It had made sense. And even though she still felt as if she should have tried harder, she'd taken Taneka's advice and gone out that evening—to the party where she'd met Greg.

The man she'd married and recently divorced.

But even Greg hadn't pointed a finger at Carly and blamed her for the breakup of their marriage.

"I want someone who really cares about me," he'd told her, "someone I can be myself with."

Of course, at first she'd been stunned. She'd done everything she could do to make sure he had a home and a wife he could be proud of, so his rejection had crushed her.

She'd felt like a failure, yet she knew no one could have tried harder than she had. And that realization began to spike her anger.

Come to think of it, she'd been spending way too much time stewing in her own sorrow, blaming herself for not being able to give Greg what he'd needed. But *he'd* failed *her,* too.

Like Greg, Carly had wanted to be married to someone who truly cared about her. Someone who wouldn't give up on a relationship.

Rather than beat herself up anymore, she decided then and there to do something positive—at least as far as Rachel was concerned.

"I was thinking," Carly told the girl. "If I wanted to take you to visit a real gym, where they offer lessons to kids who want to go to the Olympics someday, who should I talk to? Who do I need to ask for permission?"

Rachel's jaw dropped nearly to the ground, and her eyes widened. "You mean Mrs. Stafford?"

"No. We'd probably go on a Saturday. So I need to talk to someone at your house."

"I guess Erika. I'm staying with her until my mom gets back."

"All right. When would be a good time to reach her?"

Rachel shrugged. "Erika works a lot."

"Maybe I can give you my cell phone number and ask her to call me whenever it's convenient."

"Okay."

Carly excused herself to go into the office and write a note to Rachel's guardian. She'd been tempted to tell the child what she really had up her sleeve—that she'd like to enroll her in gymnastics classes and make sure she was able to get back and forth to the gym—but Carly kept those details to herself.

What if she built up Rachel's hopes only to have Erika say no?

That disappointment might be too hard for anyone to bounce back from.

After handing the note to Rachel and watching her tuck it into her pocket, Carly joined Lulu and the other girls in a game of freeze tag.

The rest of the afternoon passed before she knew it. And as she and Lulu walked out of the center together, they paused in the parking lot, next to Lulu's car, an old-style, flamingo-pink VW bug with bright yellow rims and shiny, black armorized tires.

The vehicle seemed to fit a young college student with a flashy but haphazard wardrobe.

Lulu opened the passenger door and removed a pair of black boots from the seat. Then she balanced herself on first one foot, then the other, as she removed the high-top tennies and replaced them with something more stylish.

"Stan and I are going to the Concert on the Green down at the park this evening," she told Carly. "It's a bluegrass jamboree."

As in fiddles, banjos and a lively down-home beat?

Carly couldn't help thinking it was some kind of joke and she'd missed the punch line. "Are you kidding?"

"No." Lulu tottered and braced herself against the side of the car while she slipped into a second boot. "Why do you say that?"

"The bluegrass music, I suppose. I'm from Texas, and I've always liked it. But you don't seem to be the type who would."

"I'm not what you'd call a fan, but Stan's a musician and pretty eclectic in his taste. I go just to keep him company."

With hair the color of straw and styled in a brush cut, Stan was a quiet, ordinary sort. But apparently there was a lot more to the young man than met the eye.

On the other hand, Lulu, who'd dyed her hair orange over the weekend, had a soulful wistfulness, gave off a girls-just-want-to-have-fun vibe and seemed to travel to the beat of her own eclectic band.

Together they made an interesting couple.

"So what's up with you and Bo?" Lulu asked.

"Excuse me?"

"Are you dating?"

"No. Why?"

Lulu shrugged. "Just wondered. I heard he had his eye on you at the party Saturday night."

He did?

Carly's senses soared, and she nearly asked Lulu for more details. *What did you see? What did he do?* she wanted to ask. But Lulu and Stan had been patrolling the outside of the building when Carly and Bo had gone indoors. "Who told you that?"

"A couple of little preteen birdies. You've become a novelty around here."

Carly was a novelty?

And Lulu *wasn't?*

For a woman who'd fought long and hard to be accepted by the Bannings and their high-society crowd, Carly wasn't into making bold statements, especially with her hair and clothing. And even though she admired Lulu's I-don't-give-a-rat's-hind-end attitude about what others might think, she didn't understand why the girls would consider *her* a novelty.

"What are you talking about?"

"You haven't caught wind of the giggles and whispers?"

Carly shook her head.

"With your blond hair, blue eyes and trendy wardrobe, they see you as some kind of fairy princess."

Lulu laughed as though there was something comical about it all and Carly wasn't getting it. "They've been calling you Barbie," she added. "You're their own walking, talking, life-size doll."

Carly didn't know whether she should be embarrassed or flattered. "Silly kids."

"Yep," Lulu said, as she tossed her red tennies into the passenger seat, then circled the bug to climb behind the wheel. "And they've been referring to Bo as Ken."

As in Ken and Barbie?

That was wild.

Still, Carly couldn't help fantasizing about the handsome hunk who knew how to have fun and related so well with children. He'd make a nice husband for someone, a great dad for his kids.

A great Ken doll for the right Barbie.

That night, after Carly had climbed into bed and was drifting off to sleep, the phone rang.

She picked it up on the second ring. "Hello?"

"Carly Alderson?"

"Yes."

"This is Erika Langley, Rachel's guardian."

"Oh, yes," Carly said, throwing back the covers, sitting up and swinging her legs over the side of the bed. "I'm so glad you called."

"Rachel gave me your note."

"She said you're pretty busy, so I thought this might be the best way to talk." Carly combed her fingers through her hair, trying to clear the sleep from her mind. "I really haven't discussed this with her. But I know how much she'd like to take gymnastics classes. I'm also willing to pay for it and transport her."

"What's the catch?" Erika asked.

"There isn't one."

Silence filled the line, and Carly didn't know if she should continue talking or give Erika time to think.

"Those lessons are expensive," the woman said. "Claudia, my oldest, took ballet for a while. She enjoyed it while it lasted."

When Carly was a child, there hadn't been money for extras. And she would have loved to have someone provide something like that for her. "I've been fortunate and can afford to help, so I'd like to pay for the lessons for Rachel. That is, if you'll let me."

"I guess there isn't any harm in that."

"Then would it be all right if I picked her up on Saturday and took her to the gym?"

"Yeah. But not this Saturday. She's going on that camping trip sponsored by the community center."

The camping trip Bo had talked about?

Carly had thought it was only for the boys, although it made sense that the girls would be going, too.

"Aren't you a part of that trip?" Erika asked.

Carly hadn't even considered it. She appreciated her pillow-top mattress too much. But maybe she should give it some thought. "I'm not sure yet, but if they need an additional chaperone, I'll go."

"Well, I know a lot of you down at the center are volunteers, and I appreciate the time you put in. Even before Marianne, Carly's mom, left her with me, I've had to work two jobs to make ends meet. And my girls are teenagers now and busy with their friends. So when Rachel isn't at the center, she stays home alone a lot of the time."

Unsupervised?

"How long have you been looking out for her?" Carly asked.

"About a year now. I don't have any idea what happened to her mother. We were friends back when we were in high school, but I hadn't seen her in years. Then one day she called me out of the blue and asked me to take Rachel for a couple of weeks." Erika paused, then sucked in a slow, deep breath, as though inhaling smoke from a cigarette and savoring the taste. Then, finally, she slowly blew it out.

"Obviously you agreed," Carly said.

"Yes, thinking it was a temporary situation. But then Marianne called about a month later and said she needed a little more time to get her life situated."

"Do you have any idea when she'll be back?"

"Not a clue," Erika said. "Marianne was always pretty self-centered. I'd hoped she'd grown up some after having a kid, but it doesn't look like it."

"Does she help you with support?"

"Hell no," the woman said. "I got a whopping twenty bucks when she dropped her off. And then she promised to send me a money order in the mail. But of course I haven't seen squat."

"Have you called the authorities?"

"No. But I'm thinking about it. I've been pedaling as fast as I can to pay the rent and feed everyone. In the back of my mind, I keep thinking Marianne will come back. But I haven't heard from her in ages. And my hopes of her ever coming back are fading fast."

The poor kid.

"Does Rachel miss her mother?"

"It's hard to believe, but she doesn't seem to. She cried some at first. But not so much anymore." Erika paused, and Carly could hear what sounded like a long swallow and ice cubes clinking against glass. "Marianne never did seem like the maternal type, if you know what I mean."

Carly could only imagine. At least her mother had loved her and would never have dumped her on a friend so she could get her act together, or whatever it was Marianne was doing.

"Rachel's a good kid," Erika said. "She doesn't give me any trouble."

Again Carly suspected the girl wasn't one to complain. "Thanks for letting me provide her with gymnastics lessons."

"Yeah, well, thanks for the offer. Lord knows I don't have much time for her."

"I'm sure you're doing the best you can."

At least Carly hoped so.

Because if Erika wasn't doing her best? If Rachel wasn't being cared for?

Carly would have to do something about it, although she wasn't quite sure what.

On Wednesday afternoon, Bo pulled into the parking lot of the South Rosewood Community Center just as Carly arrived.

He suspected things would be a little awkward between them, which didn't sit well with him. Over the past couple of weeks, they'd shared a few smiles and tender moments and had...

Well, he supposed they'd grown comfortable with each other.

But after he'd nearly kissed her on Saturday night, he'd been forced to admit there was something else going on between them, something sexual simmering under the surface. And it left him in a position that was too vulnerable for his comfort zone.

So the only thing to do had been to pull back. To put some distance between them.

Not that he meant to avoid her completely. But he'd known up front that there was a possibility her ex-husband would realize he'd made a mistake by leaving her.

How could he not?

Carly was proving that she had a lot of depth to go along with that pretty face and dynamite shape. And after living with her for seven years, Greg had to know that better than anyone. So for that reason Bo was determined to keep his relationship with Carly platonic and uncomplicated, which would save them all a lot of grief down the road.

And his efforts had seemed to be working, at least until he realized she'd begun to withdraw, too.

His first clue came when she'd offered him only coffee when he'd arrived at her house on Monday. It wasn't like she owed him those yummy baked treats, but why had she gone through so much trouble for a couple of mornings in a row, then stopped abruptly?

And that wasn't all.

When he'd first started working for her, before her divorce, she never used to run errands before noon. But every day this week she'd practically taken off from the house the minute he'd arrived.

Was she finding things to keep her busy while he worked on the bookshelf in her den?

It seemed that way.

And he ought to be happy about it, relieved to have gotten off without getting himself into a sticky situation.

But for some dumb reason the gradual loss of something he couldn't put his finger on was unsettling.

He wouldn't let on that it bothered him, though. Nor would he act like anything was amiss.

So he puttered around near his truck until she'd exited her car, and then he waved and made his way toward her. "How's it going?"

"You mean here?"

It didn't really matter where. But he nodded. "Yeah."

"It's going very well."

Together they walked toward the entrance to the center as if he hadn't touched her on Saturday night, as if their gazes hadn't locked. As if a warm, tingly rush hadn't raced through his veins, and something almost magical hadn't settled between them.

But just walking next to her, seeing her in a pair of jeans and a simple blue top, made all that hocus-pocus start up again.

A heavy feeling settled over him, and he tried his best to ignore it. "From what I've heard, you have a real knack with the kids."

"Thanks. They bring something out in me, and I'm finding my niche. In fact, I've even come up with a few ideas about how and what I can contribute. And I'm not just talking about financial ways."

"What do you mean?"

"For one thing, I'm going to start up an informal girls club." She turned and flashed a smile, one that came from deep within, where she'd hidden the real Carly. "You were right, Bo. Focusing on others who are less fortunate has helped me to sleep much better at night."

Good for her. Too bad he couldn't claim the same nocturnal rest himself.

Ever since that almost-kiss on Saturday night, the pheromones dancing in the evening air and the whisper of her scent had followed him home. And he'd had a hell of a time falling to sleep, which was something he'd never admit.

"I'm glad you took my advice," he said instead. "It seems to have worked out well for everyone involved."

He opened the door for her, allowing her to enter the center first and catching another whiff of her springtime scent that gave him such a rush.

"Did you finish the bookshelf today?" she asked.

"Yes. Just before lunch."

She hadn't been there when he'd left, so he'd locked up as she'd asked him to.

"Let me know how much I owe you," she said.

"I left an invoice on the coffee table in the den, but there's no rush for you to pay me."

Upon entering, they spotted Evie at the reception desk, placing a bandage on Ronnie's elbow. The maternal woman glanced up from dishing out TLC, and when her gaze landed on Carly and Bo, relief splashed across her face. "It's good to see you two. We're shorthanded on the playground today. Lulu called in sick, and Stan is coming in later today. Brenda's outside with the kids now, but she's due for a break."

"All right." Without thinking about what he was doing, Bo placed a hand on Carly's shoulder, ready to usher her down the hall and to the back door. But her feet seemed to take root.

"You go on," she said. "I need to talk to Helen for a minute. I'll join you outside in a bit."

"Is there a problem?" he asked, kicking himself for voicing his curiosity, and letting his hand drop back where it belonged.

"I want to talk to her about taking Rachel to gymnastics lessons. And I was going to ask her about the camping trip this weekend."

"What about it?" he asked.

"Do you need any more adults to go?"

"We're covered. Why?"

"I thought it might be fun."

Carly? The ultimate girlie girl?

What if she got sunburned or rubbed up against one of several skin-irritating plants that caused an itchy rash?

Good grief. And even if Mother Nature went easy on her, there were a ton of other things she'd have to deal with in the rustic facilities.

The showers and toilets were fine, as far as he was concerned, but she was bound to be a heck of a lot more particular than he and the kids were about that sort of thing.

And what about the old army cots and worn-out mattresses they would place their bedding on? It beat sleeping on the ground, which never bothered him, either. But visions of the princess and the pea began to flash in his head.

There was no way around it. He had to talk her out of it. If she went, he was sure she'd regret it. And that meant *he'd* regret her coming along, too. "Camping with the kids will be pretty rugged, Carly. You won't enjoy it."

"Why not?"

"We aren't really roughing it at Rowan's Pond, since there are cabins and bunk beds to sleep in, but for someone like you, it'd be a long, painful weekend."

"Someone like me?" She lifted a brow and crossed her arms, clearly taking offense at something he'd only meant as a friendly warning.

Common sense told him to backpedal, to apologize and let the subject drop. But he couldn't seem to let it go. "This trip will be more rugged than you're used to, and I'm only trying to look out for you. What if you come back with a broken nail or covered with mosquito bites?"

"Are you trying to scare me?" she asked. "If so, it's having the opposite effect."

Crap. He hadn't expected her to bristle and decide to prove she could handle rustic living conditions. "It's just that—"

"Forget it," she snapped. "If Helen okays it, I'm going, Bo. And I'll show you what kind of woman I really am."

That's what he was afraid of.

An unbidden picture of Carly popped into his head—freshly showered, wearing a white sundress and standing barefoot in a mountain meadow. She looked as vulnerable as a doe, yet sweeter and more touchable than she had a right to be.

But he shook the vision from his mind.

"Whatever," he said. "I just thought you'd be a lot more comfortable at home. That's all."

As he headed to the playground, he realized it really wasn't her comfort on the trip he was worried about.

It was his own.

Chapter Nine

After talking to Helen, Carly learned that Lulu had been rushed to the hospital last night, suffering from appendicitis. And since she'd be recovering from emergency surgery for a while, she wouldn't be able to take part in the camping trip.

So Carly's offer to go to Rowan's Pond in her place received Helen's wholehearted approval, not to mention her appreciation.

"By the way," Carly added, "I've enrolled Rachel in a gymnastics class for beginners. I've told Erika Langley, her guardian, and have her permission. So we'll start a week from Saturday."

"Does Rachel know?"

"Not yet. But I can hardly wait to tell her. She's going to be thrilled."

"I'm sure she will. And just knowing she has someone in her corner, someone who believes in her, could make all the difference in the world for her when she hits the teen years."

"There's something else I'd like to do for her," Carly said, not sure how Helen would react to her latest idea. One she'd gotten last night after thoughts of Bo had wakened her, and she'd gone into the kitchen for a cup of tea and tried to get her mind on something else.

"What's that?" Helen asked.

"I don't know if you've noticed or not, but Rachel wears the same outfit several days in a row. I'm not sure whether that's because no one in the house encourages her to bathe or put on fresh clothing, or if it's because the laundry doesn't get done very often and she doesn't have many clothes to choose from. Either way, I get the idea that the household budget is tight, so I want to take her shopping to buy a few things."

"I don't see a problem with it."

"Well, there could be a negative repercussion," Carly said. "I've been trying to draw her out and encourage her to make friends with the other girls, but if they decide that Rachel is my pet, it could create more problems for her."

"You've got a point."

"So I came up with a way around that."

Helen leaned back in her desk chair, her eyes bright

and a smile tugging at her lips. "You're certainly proving to be a lot more resourceful than most of our volunteers, Carly. How do you plan to pull that off?"

"I thought I'd take all the girls shopping. And when I get an idea what size she wears and the colors she likes, I can go back and get a couple additional outfits later."

"When do you want to take them?"

"Well, if it's okay with parents and guardians, maybe tomorrow. I'm not scheduled to work here on Thursdays, so that shouldn't be a problem, unless Lulu's surgery has left you shorthanded and you need me to cover."

"With the girls going with you, we'll be all right. But have you thought about transportation? One of the larger items on my wish list for the center is a used bus, but so far we don't have anyone willing to donate such a thing."

"I could rent one of those extra-large vans," Carly said. "And I'd pay for it, of course."

"That works for me. But let me talk to my husband first. He has some pull with members of the Chamber of Commerce, as well as the Kiwanis and other community service groups. He might know someone willing to loan us a vehicle for a couple of hours. Also, I'll need to call the parents and get permission for the outing. I can't imagine any of them not appreciating your kind offer."

"That would be great. Thanks."

As Carly headed out to the playground, her thoughts again turned to Bo, and she felt compelled to search for him, to see him. To know where he was and what he was doing.

It was childish, she realized, and just the kind of thing a preadolescent girl with a crush on a boy would do. And it was just plain silly to be so curious about a man who didn't seem interested in anything more than friendship.

But ever since he'd nearly kissed her on Saturday night, Carly had tried to avoid him, tried to keep to herself and not let him sense how disappointed she'd been that he hadn't kissed her—a game plan that led to her stretching the truth about her sleeping habits.

It hadn't been an out-and-out lie. She *had* been sleeping better since volunteering her time at the center. But ever since Saturday, fantasies of Bo had haunted her, slipping into her dreams.

And each night since then, Bo took her in his arms and kissed her senseless, their hands groping, hearts pounding, breaths growing ragged.

Wasn't that wild, when she'd never actually experienced the feel of his lips, the taste of him?

The dreams had been pure fantasies.

Fantasies that had surpassed any she'd ever had about Greg.

Before she could reprimand herself further, a voice shrieked from the playground, followed by, "Yay! Look, everybody. Carly's here."

Her gaze followed the sound of the young voice, and she spotted Kylie Willett seated at the top of the slide.

The little blonde quickly slid down, her feet landing on the soft grass, then skipped toward Carly, the other girls not far behind.

Well, everyone but Rachel, who stood near the swing set and appeared curious yet cautious.

That's okay, Carly told herself. It would take time for Rachel to warm up to the others. Time for her to feel safe enough to do so.

The rest of the afternoon progressed as normal, just the usual I-had-it-first and it's-not-my-fault tiffs. For the most part, Carly and Bo were wrapped up in their own activities, but that didn't mean she wasn't able to watch him from a distance, to be moved by the way the boys looked up to him.

And a couple of times she caught him doing the same thing—watching her from across the playground.

What was it with him?

Those dang mixed messages he sent were doing a real number on her.

Maybe he was still bumfuzzled about her wanting to go camping with the group.

Okay, so roughing it in mountain cabins and sleeping on cots was probably going to be too rustic for her. And when she'd volunteered to go along, she'd surprised herself, too.

Had it really been her who'd had that me-oh-please-pick-me attitude toward trekking out into the great outdoors?

Maybe so. But she chalked it up to feeling as if she

was missing something in her life. Something Bo had probably been born with.

Still, for someone who preferred spending her weekends at a five-star resort, where the maids turned down the sheets each night and left Godiva chocolates on pillows, Bo's comments about what she could expect at Rowan's Pond should have convinced her to back down gracefully and stick around Rosewood this weekend.

But oh, no.

Instead, Carly and her big mouth had threatened to show him what she was made of, which, to be honest, she was still trying to figure out. But it seemed as though he'd thrown down an are-you-a-woman-or-a-mouse gauntlet, and for some dumb reason, she refused to admit to having a cheese-nibbling, whisker-twitching side.

She was probably setting herself up for a mighty big fall, but each day she spent at the center with kids who looked up to her, people who appreciated her, she grew more confident, more competent.

And not as quick to fuss about a broken nail or any other little inconvenience that might have been a major crisis before.

Yet even with her budding self-confidence, she couldn't deny the feelings Bo stirred in her. And she wasn't just talking about the need to prove herself.

For some dumb reason, she was looking forward to spending the weekend with him more than she cared to admit.

Broken nails, mosquito bites and dirt be damned.

* * *

On Wednesday evening, Carly drove to the sporting goods store at the shopping plaza and purchased a sleeping bag and a variety of other camping necessities an enthusiastic teenage clerk suggested she buy.

As she packed her purchases in the back of her Mercedes, she spotted a clothing store she hadn't paid any attention to before. One she'd heard about, but never would have frequented.

Felice's Nieces, a trendy boutique for tweens—the gangly preadolescents who fell between the cute little girl stage and full-blown teenagers—boasted a brightly colored display in each of two windows that flanked the front door.

What a stroke of luck.

Forget taking the girls to the mall, where it might be hard to control a group of ten to twelve. Felice's Nieces would be a perfect alternative, Carly realized.

So when Thursday afternoon rolled around, that's just where she told them they were going.

After being assured that each respective parent or guardian had granted permission for the trip, Carly opened the side door of an eleven-seat van Helen had borrowed and watched ten little girls pile inside.

"Buckle up," she told them, as she slid behind the wheel and secured her own seat belt.

Then she started the engine. Before pulling out of the parking lot, she turned on the radio, tuned in a popular rock station and adjusted the volume louder than she had in years.

"I love this song," one of the girls said.

"Me, too."

And soon Carly was serenaded by her pint-size passengers. Their enthusiasm was contagious, and she couldn't help but join the off-key chorus.

Several songs later, she pulled in front of Felice's Nieces, much to the delight of her passengers. And once they got out of the van, the girls practically bounced through the door in true Tigger fashion.

Even Rachel, who took up the rear and was subdued compared to the others, perked up upon entering the boutique, where the first thing that caught everyone's eye was a plasma screen TV playing the latest Britney Spears concert DVD in surround sound.

After scanning the shop in awe, the girls swarmed around a table in front that displayed a variety of summer wear, including shorts and T-shirts in a kaleidoscope of colors. Then, one by one, they made their way to the carousels of clothes.

The manager, Bonnie Lindstrom, introduced herself to Carly, adding, "It sure looks like you've got your hands full."

"I think we'll both be busy with them," Carly replied with a smile. "I'll be buying them each a new outfit."

Two hours later, the girls giggled and chattered as they waited at one of the registers for Bonnie to tally up the sale and Carly to hand over a credit card.

The kids had each thanked Carly profusely, making her glad she'd been able to treat them. In fact, she looked forward to doing it again someday.

Kylie, a blonde in pigtails, tapped Carly's arm. "This is *so* cool. You're the man."

"Wouldn't that be *woman?*" Shawna asked.

"Aw, she knows what I mean."

They all laughed, warming her heart once again.

But it was the way Rachel reverently held the new lavender skirt and matching blouse to her chest that made Carly realize it truly was more blessed to give than to receive.

And as Rachel took a seat next to Shawna and Kylie, her beaming smile only drove the concept home, compelling Carly to leave all her young charges in the van—locking them in securely, of course—while she returned to the store.

"One of the girls had a tough time choosing between several outfits," Carly told Bonnie. "The green-and-white-striped skirt and coordinating top was one of them. And the jeans with the embroidered ladybug and the red T-shirt was the other. They were both size eights."

"Are you talking about the little girl with her brown hair in a ponytail? The one you followed around the store?"

Carly's heart dropped, and her fears of what the other girls might say or do if they thought she had a favorite tumbled around in her stomach. "Was I that noticeable?"

"Only to me. The kids were too caught up in their excitement. And I can understand why. It appeared that most of the clothing they wore in here had been handed down a couple of times."

"Will you do me a favor?" Carly asked.

"Certainly."

"Can you please hold those outfits for me? I realize you'll be closing soon, but I'll try to come back tomorrow sometime."

"Of course. And I'm also going to refigure that sales slip and credit your card twenty-five percent."

Carly had done a heck of a lot of shopping in her time, but she'd never had a store manager offer something like that. "Why?"

"There's a joy in giving, and let's just say I'd like to do my part, too."

Bonnie was right. There was a real perk to the benefactor who helped someone less fortunate. And Carly had received far more today than she'd given.

Yet it still didn't feel like she'd done enough.

Not for Rachel.

But what more could she do?

On Friday evening, Bo, Carly and seventeen children—nine boys and eight girls—climbed onto a borrowed bus that had been retired by the local school district. Helen's husband had also been able to find a driver who would take them and their gear to Rowan's Pond and return for them at noon on Sunday.

It hadn't taken too long to reach the campsite. And

after getting their cabin and bunk assignments, they made their beds—Carly with the girls and Bo with the boys.

Dinner was next on the schedule, and on their way to the mess hall, Carly filed in behind Shawna and Kylie, inseparable best friends who obviously hadn't realized she was so close.

"Ken's got a crush on Barbie," Kylie said in a singsong voice.

"Yeah, I know. You can *totally* tell."

How? Carly wanted to ask, but she certainly couldn't morph into preadolescent mode and dig for details.

"He looks at her all the time," Shawna said. "But that's 'cause she's so pretty. When I grow up, I hope I have boobies like hers."

"Maybe they'll be as big as Mrs. Stafford's." Kylie, who was obviously in a silly mood, began to sing, "Do your boobies hang low? Do they wobble to and fro?"

Carly decided that was her cue to slip into chaperone mode, and she tapped the girl on the shoulder.

When Kylie turned, the big smile plastered on her face faded instantly.

"You have a lovely voice, Kylie. But if you're stuck on that tune, I'd rather you sang about ears hanging low." Carly tugged gently on the girl's pigtails. "Or maybe even braids?"

"What's wrong with boobs?" Shawna asked. "It's not a bad word."

"Breasts are a lovely part of a woman and not something we should joke about. Okay?"

"Sorry."

The girls increased their pace, as if to get out of adult hearing range, and Shawna elbowed Kylie, then whispered something that sounded a lot like, "You're so dumb."

Dinner was loud but uneventful, and the food was barely tolerable. The macaroni and cheese had come from a box, and as far as Carly was concerned, the hot dogs were just salty, protein-laced fillers. But the kids seemed happy with it.

She, on the other hand, went light on the starchy carbs and tried to fill up on the apple slices provided.

After dinner they played relay-type games, with the girls against the boys. For the most part, everyone had a good time, other than two minor incidences.

Nate had a verbal tussle with Ronnie that looked as though it might escalate, but Bo took him aside, which seemed to solve the problem. And Kylie made a fuss over a tiny scratch, which Carly took care of by using the first aid kit Helen had sent along, and providing a bandage that really wasn't necessary.

Over the course of the evening, Carly made it a point not to give any credence to the whole Barbie-Ken thing. At least, she tried not to.

They retired to the cabins at nine, but it took nearly two hours for the girls to wind down and fall asleep. And then one more for Carly to realize she could expect to toss and turn on a lumpy mattress for most of the night.

Ken's got a crush on Barbie, Kylie had said.

Oh, yeah? Well, Carly was just realizing, and finally

ready to admit to herself, that Barbie had a heck of a crush on Ken. But she'd be darned if she wanted the kids to suspect how big it had gotten.

All she needed was to become fodder for a pint-size rumor mill.

Tired of staring at the glow of a night-light on the dark ceiling, she finally climbed from her sleeping bag, slid into a pair of slippers, slipped on a robe, then carefully tiptoed to the door. She had no intention of straying any distance from the cabin while the girls slept. But it certainly wouldn't hurt for her to sit on the porch for a while.

She let herself out quietly, then stood on the wood-slat flooring and peered out into the night.

The moon was nearly full, and the sky was clear, boasting a jillion diamondlike stars, winking and blinking.

The crickets were out tonight in full chorus, and down by Rowan's Pond, which was actually a respectable-size lake, a bullfrog called to its mate.

In spite of the crummy food and lodging, she decided, this had to be the best part of camping. The night sounds of nature. The crisp mountain air.

Across the way, only thirty feet or so, a porch floorboard from the boys' cabin creaked, and a shadow lurked near the window.

She squinted to make out who might be planning an escape.

The size and bulk told her it wasn't a child.

Bo?

It had to be.

Apparently he hadn't been able to sleep, either. Did he realize they were on different porches, facing each other and separated by a stretch of grass?

They stood like that awhile, silent and watchful.

Wistful, maybe?

For some reason an old song came to mind, a true golden oldie about Running Bear and Little White Dove, two Indian lovers separated by a raging river.

Oh, brother. She'd been stewing in silence for too long, and her mind was playing stupid games with her.

Still, she looked at Bo again, wondering if he would like some adult conversation.

She could use some for a change.

Would he make the first move, like Running Bear?

Probably not.

Yet although expected, his inaction seemed to be a challenge, a dare. And in spite of herself, Carly stepped off the porch, hoping she wouldn't drown— like in the song.

At least not alone.

When Carly opened the door to her cabin and stood on the porch in a white robe, Bo had been sorely tempted to join her, to ask how she liked the camp so far.

But he'd also been hard-pressed to make any kind of move.

She was untouchable. She'd let him know from the get-go that she wanted her husband back. And if the guy was contacting her, then maybe that's what was in the cards.

Who was Bo to step in and complicate things?

Sure, Greg had left her and recently started dating someone else. But he'd called her at least once since then. Maybe more than that. So there was obviously some reason he wanted to stay connected to her.

Bo had grown up in a loving family and had been taught to believe in the sanctity of marriage and that divorce shouldn't be an option. That's why he vowed he would think long and hard before promising to love someone until death parted them.

But tell that to his libido, especially since he'd begun to see Carly in a whole new light.

A blood-stirring light.

Now he was watching her make her way across the lawn, coming right toward him. The moonlight cast a silvery aura on her hair, making her look angelic in that flowing white cotton robe she wore.

"I see you can't sleep, either," she whispered, as she drew near.

Just as quietly, he replied, "Ronnie snores something fierce."

That wasn't a lie, but it wasn't the full truth, either. There'd been more than a nasally rattle that had Bo outside, watching the cabin where Carly had turned in for the night.

"Are we still on for dinner Sunday evening?" she asked. "Or did you forget I'd invited you and that you'd accepted?"

He tossed her a crooked grin. "I didn't forget. But

maybe you ought to wait and see if you're still up for it. You might be soaking blisters by then. Or smearing calamine lotion all over yourself."

"Give me a break," she said. "I can handle this trip and any of the inconveniences."

"For some reason, the fact that you're here makes me think you probably can."

"Good. I'm glad that's settled." She tossed him a smile, then combed her fingers through her hair, a shimmering blond veil made silver by the moon. "So dinner will be ready at six, if you're still interested."

His conscience was tripping all over itself, trying to convince him to decline politely, to tell her something had come up. But if her baking skills were proof, she had to be one heck of a cook.

"Six works for me," he said, blaming his agreement on hunger, even though he feared there was another hunger begging to be sated.

Carly continued forward, stepping up onto the porch, reaching for the railing.

"Ow." She jerked back her hand, then stuck the tip of her index finger in her mouth.

"What happened?"

She slid her finger out long enough to say, "I got a splinter," then slipped it in again.

He stepped closer, watching carefully.

As her eyes met his, her lips parted and her damp finger slid from her mouth once more.

Damn.

It was all so innocent. The sharp poke to her finger, the instinctive reaction to place it in her mouth.

But the sensual way her lips moved as her finger slid in…and out…

Whew.

Those pretty eyes locked on him. Pleading for something.

If he'd ever flashed one of those stunned, possum-in-the-headlights stares, it was now.

"What's the matter?" she asked.

"Nothing." He'd be damned if he'd admit what was going on in his mind. What was happening inside. Where his blood was rushing, hard and fast.

"Bo?" She placed her uninjured hand on his cheek.

He didn't move. Heck, he couldn't even speak, other than squawk out, "Yeah?"

"Kiss me."

A war between his conscience and his libido raged, and he had no clue of the outcome.

Until she turned the tide.

Her fingers slid around to the back of his neck, pulling him, drawing his mouth to hers.

Dammit, Carly.

He wasn't sure if he'd voiced the words or not, but it didn't matter. All he could do was take her in his arms and lose himself in her kiss.

Chapter Ten

A force Bo had yet to reckon with raced through his blood as he took what Carly offered, giving her all he had in return.

Her lips parted, allowing his tongue to touch hers, to seek every nook and cranny of her mouth. As he kissed her deeply and thoroughly, he couldn't seem to get enough.

She tasted of apples and magic, of wicked temptations and dreams come true. And he relished every heated touch, every ragged breath.

The kiss deepened, and he claimed her in a way he had no business doing. But that didn't seem to bother her in the least, for she leaned into him, pressing her soft breasts against his chest, shifting her pelvic bone against his growing erection, taunting him with something that could never be his.

His conscience, a small voice that had been banished to the far corners of his mind, begged him to stop. To remember who Carly was. Where they were.

To remind him why they were here.

Yet he couldn't seem to yield to common sense. Not yet. Not until he'd tasted her just this one time.

It was Carly who came to her senses first, Carly who placed her hands on his chest and pushed slowly, drawing her mouth from his.

Her breath was ragged, and her knees buckled slightly. She gripped the front of his shirt as though she needed to hold on to something. "I wish we were anywhere but here."

So did he.

His bed at home would have been nice.

But he couldn't quite deal with the heat, the reality of what they'd done, the step they'd taken that would change their friendship forever.

Friends didn't kiss each other like that.

"I'm sorry," he said, for lack of anything better to say.

And he *was* sorry. For the complications that were sure to result from that arousing kiss.

"Don't be. I wanted it to happen." She combed a hand through her hair. "I was curious."

Oh, yeah?

If truth be told, he'd been curious, too. And the kiss had gone beyond anything he could have possibly imagined.

Hell, he only meant to be her friend, only meant to help her get her husband back, yet he couldn't deny the chemistry that was developing between them or the need and desire her kiss triggered. Neither could he deny his belief that marriage was a lifetime commitment. Too many people jumped into it too quickly. But just as many bailed out too soon.

Being honest now, telling her he'd been curious, too, wasn't going to do either one of them any good. Neither was telling her that she'd turned his hormones on end.

They'd made a mistake. A big one. And he wasn't going to take advantage of her loneliness, her vulnerability.

There was only one way out of it, as far as he could see.

"Am I the first guy you've kissed since Greg?" he asked.

She nodded.

A part of him wanted to know how his kiss compared with Greg's. But he wouldn't put himself in that position.

"Weren't you a little curious about what kissing me would be like?" she asked.

He shrugged. "I guess. But now that we've got that out of the way, what do you say we head back to the little rascals we're supposed to be watching over?"

"All right." She fingered the lapel of her robe, clearly not ready to hightail it back to her cabin.

"Come on, Carly. It was just a simple kiss. It didn't mean anything."

But his conscience wasn't buying it.

He just hoped she would.

* * *

As Carly headed back to her cabin, all hope for sleep had disappeared—banished by Bo's embrace, by his blood-stirring kiss and his ultimate dismissal.

It didn't mean anything.

At least that's what he'd said.

But something inside her didn't believe him. The kiss they'd shared had nearly turned her knees to mush. And she had every reason to believe it had turned him inside out, too.

Yet for some reason he didn't want it to.

As she climbed onto the porch, she turned and glanced over her shoulder, spotted Bo standing outside.

His eyes were still fixed on her.

His thoughts, too?

Something told her they were, and she could understand why. Their friendship had taken a heated turn.

For nearly a week she'd been wondering about his kiss, wishing he wouldn't have changed his mind last Saturday night.

She'd suspected he'd felt it, too—desire, passion. Or just plain old sexual curiosity.

Still, he'd been a perfect gentleman, which had frustrated her no end. So even though she'd felt more nervous than she ever had in her life, she'd been determined to get that kiss she felt he owed her, and make the first move.

And whew.

What a kiss.

She hadn't been disappointed.

Kissing Bo in the flesh had proved to be so much more thrilling and arousing that it had been in her dreams.

It didn't mean anything, he'd said. But there was more than lust behind a kiss like that. And she knew it had meant something to him, too.

But what was she going to do? Call him a liar?

She carefully and quietly let herself into the cabin, then climbed back into her sleeping bag. And this time, when sleep finally came, heated dreams came, too, with Bo the leading man, his kisses no longer imagined.

They were as real as the desire to kiss him again.

Maybe it would happen Sunday evening when he came to her house for dinner.

The kids had a blast at camp, and Carly did, too, even though she broke a nail playing softball. She'd also gotten a blister on Saturday afternoon when they hiked to the lake. And who knew when the mosquitoes had stolen a couple of bites?

Neither she nor Bo talked about the kiss again.

In fact, they hardly talked at all.

As far as Carly was concerned, she'd been afraid the girls would pick up on the Barbie and Ken vibes, and she didn't want anyone stirring things up back at the center. God forbid Helen think that they'd become self-absorbed and forgotten their responsibilities.

On the way home from camp, most of the kids dozed off. And as they unloaded the bus, all Carly could think of was taking a nice hot soak in the tub, putting some aloe on her bug bites and some salve and a new bandage on the blister on her heel.

Well, that and cooking dinner for Bo.

Just as the last child climbed into a car with an older brother to return home, Bo's cell phone rang.

"Oh, shoot. Today? I forgot all about it." He raked a hand through his hair. "No. But I'll be there."

Her curiosity piqued, Carly gazed at Bo as he snapped his cell phone shut and looked her way. "Hey, I'm really sorry. But I can't have dinner with you tonight."

A little part of her wanted to challenge him, to ask whether the call had been a setup. Did he really have something he'd forgotten to do? Or had he found a convenient excuse?

But she let it drop.

It would be too easy to fall back into those pitiful old patterns, to flounder in those god-awful feelings of rejection and inadequacy.

"That's okay." She tried to conjure a smile to mask her disappointment. "Maybe another time."

"Thanks for understanding."

She shrugged, then shot him another wimpy smile that felt about as flat as a can of soda that had been open for a week. Then she finished packing her gear into the trunk of her car and drove home. Minus the radio this time. Or any background noise.

As she drove down Danbury Way, she spotted Sylvia outside her house, hauling a gift-wrapped box out to her car.

Carly slowed to a stop and rolled down her window. "Looks like someone's having a birthday."

"Yes, there's a gentleman down at Mountain View Manor who's turning eighty-five. And I've got to go to the party. Horace was supposed to come with me, but had to have a tooth pulled today. He's feeling kind of puny, so I'm going alone."

"That's too bad," Carly said.

"Would you like to come with me?" Sylvia asked. "It's not the kind of party that needs an RSVP. The more the merrier has always been our philosophy. Besides, I'd love to introduce you to some of the people at the home. If you ever tire of working with children or want to volunteer elsewhere, it's a great opportunity to fill another need."

Carly was torn. On one hand, she had the urge to soak in the hot tub, then veg out in front of the TV with a carton of rocky road ice cream. But that would be falling into the trap the old Carly had been mired in.

"I need to shower, which will take me at least thirty minutes. If you can wait, I'll join you. Otherwise, I'll go another time."

Sylvia glanced at her watch, then brightened as she looked up. "Sure. I can wait."

A part of her still wanted to spend the evening with the carton of rocky road and a spoon. But she opted for a healthier alternative, one that went with the new leaf she'd turned over, and she mustered a smile. "I'll be quick."

* * *

"The party actually starts at six," Sylvia said, as she and Carly entered the living-room-style lobby of Mountain View Manor. "But I volunteered to set up the social hall and decorate a bit. I hope you don't mind helping me."

"Of course not." Carly, who held Sylvia's present, scanned the homey, wallpapered room, where a television aired a classic Doris Day movie.

Sylvia, who carried a boxed sheet cake she'd picked up at the bakery, smiled at the fortysomething redhead who was manning the reception desk. "Hello, Margery. I've brought my neighbor to the party, but I'll have to formally introduce you two later. I've got to put this down before I drop it."

"Is that the cake?" Margery asked. "What kind is it?"

"I'm not sure," Sylvia said. "Whatever the family ordered. I just picked it up, since it was on my way."

"Then it must be chocolate with custard filling," Margery said to Sylvia's back. "That's his favorite."

"It's nice to informally meet you," Carly said before following her spry neighbor.

"Come on. It's this way." Sylvia nodded to the right, and they headed down the hall.

"If that box is awkward or too heavy," Carly said, increasing her pace, "let me carry it for you."

"No, I've got it." Sylvia slowed her steps long enough for Carly to catch up, then leaned close and whispered,

"Margery's a sweetheart, but she's a talker, and I don't have time to dawdle."

"I hope waiting for me to shower didn't create a problem."

"Not really. There were others delegated to do some of the setup, but I just want to make sure it's done. And if it's not, you can help." Sylvia continued to the end of the hall and through an open doorway, where twisted green crepe paper swooped through the room, matching the paper tablecloths.

"Well, I'll be darned." Sylvia placed the bakery box on the nearest table. "They did manage to find someone to decorate. Great. I was afraid Roy's family would arrive, and we wouldn't be ready for them."

A rainbow bouquet of helium balloons adorned a table that appeared to be reserved for the guest of honor, and behind it, a computer-generated Happy Birthday banner stretched across a bulletin board.

Sylvia proceeded to unpack the cake. "I would have preferred something frosted white and adorned with pretty sugar roses. But his family insisted on a baseball theme, which seems more fitting for a kid's birthday party, if you ask me."

Carly watched as Sylvia placed the cake by the punch bowl. "It's kind of cute, though. Apparently Roy's a big sports fan."

The cake had been frosted in various colors—brown for the infield, with white baselines, and green for the outfield. Little plastic players, most of them red, had been placed in the proper positions, and a yellow figure stood at bat. And in a patch meant to mimic a blue sky, cloudlike letters spelled out Happy Birthday Roy.

Awareness suddenly dawned.

Bo's uncle Roy lived in an intermediate care facility and loved baseball.

Could the men be one and the same?

"Come on," Sylvia said. "I want to go to the kitchen and make sure the punch has been made, then I'll introduce you to some of the people who live here."

But as they turned toward the door, a gray-haired man in a wheelchair rolled himself in. He wore a bright red vest and had a blue plaid blanket draped over his lap.

"Well, here's the man of the hour now," Sylvia said. "Happy birthday, Roy. I'd like to introduce you to Carly Alderson, my neighbor. Carly, this is Roy Conway."

"How do you do?"

"Not bad for a man pushing ninety."

"You're only eighty-five," Sylvia reminded him.

Roy stopped wheeling long enough to reach out a gnarled and liver-spotted hand to Carly.

She took it in hers, noting that he held on longer than the norm. His eyes never left hers, while he addressed her neighbor. "Now, Syl, I told you folks not to bring me a present. But since you apparently forgot, I'll just thank you and keep her."

Sylvia clucked her tongue, eyes bright with mirth. "If

I'd have brought you a woman, Roy, it would have been one more your age."

"Now what good would that do me?" he asked. "Even though they know I'm not interested, I've got to keep these wheels turning as fast as they'll go so the ladies can't catch me. And don't think some haven't tried their damnedest to bushwhack me."

Carly couldn't help but smile, liking the man instantly.

"But don't worry," he added, winking at Carly. "I'd slow down for you, honey."

Roy was a hoot.

He had to be Bo's uncle. After all, how many elderly Roy Conways lived in Rosewood *and* at Mountain View Manor?

And if she was right, the entire Conway family would show up to celebrate his birthday.

No wonder Bo had passed on having dinner at her house tonight.

Her relief was palpable, and so was her delight when she thought how surprised he'd be to see her here.

"Seems to me a pretty gal like you ought to be married or engaged or pretty damn close to it," Roy said. "I don't suppose you're free to date?"

For the very first time since Greg had mentioned a divorce, she was happy to be able to admit she was available. "Believe it or not, I'm single."

"Oh, yeah?" He arched a gray, bushy brow. "That's good, because I've got four nephews—all good boys. Hardworking. Honest. Good-looking, too." He leaned back in his wheelchair and grinned. "In case you haven't noticed, they got all that from me."

"Lucky boys," Carly said, truly believing they were, and growing more fond of their great-uncle by the minute.

"One of them, Pete, Jr., found himself one hell of a wife last spring. But the other three are up for grabs."

Carly wouldn't mind taking Bo off the market, but she'd keep that budding plan to herself awhile longer. "I didn't realize it until arriving here with Sylvia, but I might know one of your nephews already. In fact, we just returned from a weekend camping trip."

"Oh, yeah? Which boy was that?"

"Bo."

A wry grin curved the old man's face, crinkling his eyes. "If you're interested in that one, he's a keeper."

"Why?" Carly asked, wanting to know more about the talented carpenter who'd touched her heart, as well as the boy he used to be.

"For one thing, Bo's a good listener, but he's also got a quick wit and a sense of humor."

"That sounds like the man I know," she said with a smile.

"But there's more to him than that. And even when he was only a few years out of a diaper, he had a slew of common sense and the ability to learn from the mistakes of others." Roy rested his hands in his lap. "So I invested a little more time in him than I did with his brothers."

"Teaching him how to play ball?" she asked.

"Nope." The old man's hazel eyes glimmered. "They all got a fair shake when it came to sports. But I went out of my way to teach Bo all I knew about life, women, politics, business…."

"Did he listen?"

"Best I can tell. And I have to tell you, little lady. On the outside chance you might think I'm a smidgen too old for you, go ahead and set your sights on Bo. He's the one who's most like me."

"I'll have to give that some careful thought," she said, as though she hadn't already set her sights on the man. As though she hadn't begun to realize it was more than a crush she was struggling with.

Much more.

Roy glanced down at his hands, lifting the wrist that bore a gold watch. "Damn. It's getting late. I don't want to be the first one here. It makes it look as though I'm eager for all the attention."

"And you're *not?*" Sylvia asked, chuckling.

"Not that I'm willing to admit."

As Roy began to maneuver the wheelchair and turn toward the doorway, Carly volunteered to push him.

"Are you sure it won't be too much trouble?" he asked.

"It would be my pleasure." Then she turned to Sylvia. "I'll be back shortly."

"No problem. I'm going to the kitchen to check on that punch."

Carly stepped behind the wheelchair, guiding Roy

186   *THE PERFECT WIFE*

out the door. "You'll have to be the navigator. I don't know where your room is."

"Straight ahead, past the reception area. Then it's the second door on the right."

The reception desk no more than came into view when Carly glanced that way and spotted Bo talking to Margery.

He looked up, and his jaw practically dropped to the linoleum floor when he saw her. He excused himself from the red-haired receptionist, then sauntered toward them, recovering long enough to reach out a hand to his great-uncle. "Happy birthday, Roy."

"Glad you could make it, son." The elderly man looked over his shoulder. "I take it you've already met Carly."

"Yeah. We've met."

"Heard you also spent the weekend together," the old man said.

"It wasn't like that," Carly quickly explained. "We went with kids from the South Rosewood Community Center. As chaperones."

"I imagine it might have been nicer to have spent the time alone, huh?" Roy beamed sagely. "There's nothing like a little spooning under the stars."

Bo's gaze met Carly's, and she was still having trouble deciding what was going through his mind.

Was it something more than just being surprised to see her? Was he annoyed, thinking she'd crashed the party?

Just in case, she decided to set him straight. "I ran into my neighbor on the way home, and she asked if I wanted to ride with her to Mountain View Manor, since she knows

I've been volunteering in the community lately. Little did I know we'd be celebrating your uncle's birthday tonight."

"Small world," Bo said.

"I'd invited him to dinner at my house," Carly said to Roy, bypassing Bo and the uneasiness she sensed— God forbid they suffer in awkward silence. "But he had other plans tonight. I had no idea it was a family party, and that we'd end up eating birthday cake together. And speaking of cake, it looks great. And yummy."

Okay. Enough babbling and trying to make the conversation lighthearted and comfortable for everyone. If Bo had a problem with her presence, that was too darn bad.

She continued to push Roy's chair forward. To the left, they came to the open doorway of the dining room, where an elderly man spoon-fed a woman seated in a wheelchair much like Roy's. The white-haired woman wore a bib tied around her neck.

How sad.

"Looky there," Roy said, pointing toward the couple.

Carly, who suddenly wanted the linoleum to swallow her up, couldn't imagine why he would point out the poor woman's handicap.

"It tickles the hell out of me to see that," Roy went on.

To see what?

"Back up a tad," he told Carly. Then he lifted his hand to wave and raised his voice. "Hello, Hank. How's Ellen doing this evening?"

"Much better, thank you."

"Glad to hear it. Will you two be joining us for cake and ice cream?"

"If it's not too much for her. She tires easily these days." The man used a napkin to carefully wipe a dribble from the woman's chin, then added, "But we'll try to stop by."

Roy nodded, then motioned for Carly to pick up the pace.

"You don't see that in the movies," Roy said. "But that's true love. That's what it's all about. Teamwork. A commitment that will last for the long haul and not quit when life gets tough."

Carly hadn't thought about it that way, and rather than feeling complete sympathy for the woman, she felt a little envious, too. She would have given anything to have a man love her that much, to remain devoted over the years.

She and Greg hadn't had a relationship like that, and she realized that was the kind of marriage she wanted. The kind she deserved.

And next time...

Her gaze drifted to Bo again, and she found him watching her. But she'd be darned if she'd figured out what he was thinking.

Or feeling.

Chapter Eleven

Carly had been the last person in the world Bo had expected to see at Mountain View Manor tonight, the last one to be pushing Roy's wheelchair and charming the man to pieces.

But why not?

She'd been charming Bo for the past couple of weeks, too, tempting him to throw caution to the wind.

Then, when he'd kissed her, when he'd had a taste of her, desire had hit him full force, pressing him to claim her as his own. The sheer intensity of the impulse had scared the living daylights out of him. And he knew his only hope had been to pull away for good. Because if she pressed him, he'd kiss her again.

And what good would that do anyone?

Bo had seen the couple Roy had pointed out and understood why he had. Uncle Roy and Aunt Mary had shared that same kind of love.

It was also the same lifelong commitment Bo wanted to have someday and the reason he wouldn't settle for less.

His competitive streak ran deep, and as far as he was concerned, second place was just another term for loser.

And getting involved with Carly—if that's the direction their friendship was heading—would put him in a second place position, leaving him to wonder if he could ever fully compete with Greg in her heart. To wonder if she would ever be able to make a clean cut with her ex and give Bo a fighting chance.

Before he could give gambling on a relationship with her any further thought, his mom's voice called out from the lobby. "There you are!"

As the short, heavyset woman breezed past the reception desk with a stack of gifts in her arms, she headed straight for them, her cheeks flushed, her eyes glimmering. "Happy Birthday, Roy!"

She stooped to give the wheelchair-bound man a kiss, then shuffled her gifts and her purse in order to greet Bo with a one-armed hug. "Hi, honey. I had a feeling you'd beat us here."

"This lovely young lady is Carly," Roy said, twisting to peer at the blonde who stood behind his chair. "She and Bo are dating."

Bo opened his mouth to object, but his mom's bright smile nearly blinded him, and she bypassed him completely.

"That's wonderful." She reached out a hand to Carly. "I'm Marla Conway. And I'm happy to meet you."

Bo didn't normally bring his dates to meet the family, so it was easy to see how his mom might think that he and Carly were becoming serious.

But that conclusion was half-baked and premature.

"Actually, Carly came with her neighbor," Bo said.

"Either way, it's nice to have you here." His mom returned her attention to Roy. "Pete's working late, as usual. But he'll be here in time for the cake."

"I figured he would. That boy has a sweet tooth that just won't quit."

"Oh. By the way, Roy, Pete's off on Saturday, so he'll be the one picking you up this time. I'll be home cooking a big dinner—prime rib and all the fixings. So don't fill up at breakfast."

Roy nodded.

The Conways visited Roy regularly and brought him home for the holidays and weekend dinners. But Bo's dad had been working a lot of overtime lately, and it had been awhile since they'd all gotten together.

Marla turned to Bo, placed her free hand on his back and gave it a maternal caress. "Your brothers are coming, so I hope you don't already have plans."

"I wouldn't miss it."

Those Conway family dinners were special. And not just because Bo and his brothers would fill up on the mouthwatering home cooking they'd all grown up on. Getting together also gave the men a chance to be boys again. And whether they shot a few hoops, played football in the street or hung out in the garage and studied the engine of the '67 Camaro their father planned to refurbish when he retired, the day would prove to be a good one.

Bo had been wanting to introduce Nate to the men in his family, so the timing was perfect. "Do you mind if I bring a friend?"

His mom brightened again, redirecting her attention to Carly. "Of course. We'd love to have you, dear."

Oops. That wasn't what he'd meant.

"Thank you," Carly said. "Dinner on Saturday sounds great. But please let me bring something. Maybe double chocolate fudge brownies? I found a recipe I've been wanting to try."

"Normally, I'd say no, don't bring anything. But my husband is a chocoholic, so, yes. Please do."

Damn. It was definitely too late to backpedal now, but maybe there was a way to right the misunderstanding. Or at least make the family dinner seem less like a date.

"If you don't mind," Bo said to his mother, "I'd like to include one of the boys from the center, too. His name is Nate, and he's been through a lot of crap a kid shouldn't have to deal with. He's also in foster care, which is a good thing. But he could use some male role models."

"Of course, Bo. You can bring anyone you like. All you have to do is let me know so there will be plenty to eat."

Nope. That was it. He'd reached his quota.

He supposed he could have waited and taken Nate home to meet everyone another time. But now there were two reasons for the boy to come along.

First of all, Nate would get a chance to meet some great guys—a noble thing, no doubt about it. But the second reason was more self-serving.

Nate's presence would make Carly's visit seem less like a take-her-home-to-meet-the-folks thing.

Heck. All Bo needed was for Carly or his family to think they actually had a future together.

Because it was tough enough reminding himself that they didn't.

On Saturday afternoon, Bo picked up Nate at his foster home in South Rosewood, then drove to the McMansion, which would have been just plain stupid if he'd wanted to save time and gas. But even though he was going out of his way and driving back and forth across town, Bo wanted a buffer between him and Carly.

Okay. So he was a coward. But shoot, he'd never intended to bring her home to meet the family in the first place. Not yet, anyway. And the whole thing made him uneasy—especially since all the Conways seemed to hit it off with her at the birthday party.

He'd gotten elbowed by each of his brothers at least once. And he'd been winked at a couple of times. Even Jennifer, his oldest brother's wife, had taken him aside and quizzed him about where they'd met, how long they'd been dating.

Fortunately, he'd been able to skate around the truth, which was that he wasn't sure what they meant to each other or where things were going.

Still, you'd think he'd made an official announcement and Carly was now sporting a sparkling new diamond ring on her left hand.

Bo's ring.

Not Greg's.

Something he'd yet to consider settled over him, stunning him with a gut-twisting thought.

Bo could afford a nice diamond. A respectable size stone. But it wouldn't be anything as big as Greg had given her.

Yeah, yeah, yeah. Biggest didn't mean best. Money wasn't everything. It wasn't whether you won or lost, but how you played the game.

He knew all that. But ever since Petey started bringing home blue ribbons, medals and trophies, Bo had tried his best to keep up. To compete. To make a name for himself in the family, at school and in the community.

Coming in a close second had never been good

enough for Bo, and becoming the new man in Carly's life would ensure him a permanent position in the number two spot, making him her lover by default—if things actually went that far.

So he'd pretty much avoided her—and their situation—for the rest of the week.

He'd seen her again on Wednesday, when they'd worked at the center, but he'd managed to keep the conversation generic then, too. But that didn't mean he hadn't considered all the possibilities and pitfalls of a relationship with her. Or that he hadn't picked up the phone a couple of times, just to hear her voice—then had second thoughts and hung up.

It had been a hell of a long time between Wednesday and Saturday.

His gut was still twisted when he parked his pickup in the circular drive. And the coward that he was growing into asked Nate to come with him to the door.

It didn't taken much to convince the kid, though. The boys at the center had been all abuzz about the new blond volunteer, the one they called Barbie behind her back.

Bo supposed more than a couple of the boys had crushes on her, and he couldn't blame them.

After ringing the bell, he and Nate didn't have to wait long.

Carly swung open the door, wearing a simple but stylish white sundress and carrying a gray ceramic platter that was piled high with brownies and covered with plastic wrap. She stunned them both with a pretty smile, then greeted Nate first, which caused the tough guy to flush and shuffle his feet.

"I need to get my purse," she said. "Nate, can you please carry these for me?"

The red-haired boy nodded, as though struggling to find his tongue, and she handed him the goodies.

Then she cast a smile on Bo that shot straight to his heart, jump-starting his pulse and making him wonder if his cheeks were flushed the same shade as Nate's.

He figured he'd probably stammer if he tried to tell her how pretty she looked, or that he'd have to beat his single brothers off with a stick. So instead he asked if she was ready to go.

"I certainly am." She turned to grab her purse from an antique table near the door, then removed the key and locked up the house.

As they walked toward the pickup, she added, "I'm glad you invited me."

Yeah, well, he couldn't very well tell her that the invitation had been a mistake, a misunderstanding. "It's no big deal. Just a home-cooked meal and some laughs."

Nate stood beside the open passenger door, his freckled face grinning like a dapper young valet, and Carly slid in, taking the spot in the middle.

Was Nate trying to be a matchmaker? Or was he just being polite?

Either way, Bo supposed, it really didn't matter.

He'd lost a certain amount of control over this whole mess the moment his mom had assumed Carly was the friend he'd wanted to bring home.

As he climbed behind the wheel and reached for the buckle of his seat belt, his arm bumped against her shoulder, her fingers grazed his. A jolt of heat shot through him, and his hormones went berserk.

"Oops," she said, blessing him with a heart-strumming smile. "Sorry."

"No problem," he lied.

If he couldn't keep his testosterone in check, this was going to be a heck of a long day.

The drive back to South Rosewood would take about fifteen minutes, so to keep his mind off the woman beside him, the pretty knee that peered out from the hem of her dress and the thigh that warmed his, Bo cleared his throat and addressed the boy.

"So, how's it going at home, Nate? Is Fran treating you okay?"

"Yeah. She's nice."

Bo had done some checking and had learned that Fran Huddleston had been involved in foster care since the 1980s. Her husband had passed away about two years ago, but she continued to take in kids who needed a home. Her reputation was impeccable, and it seemed Nate's plight had been carefully considered when he was placed with her. Between Fran, the volunteers at the center and the men in Bo's family, they ought to be able to help the boy get his life on track.

"How's your mom?" Bo asked, hating to mention the woman who'd suffered a brutal beating at the hands of her husband and would never be the same again. Yet he didn't want to pretend she didn't exist, either. Not when Nate needed to accept and deal with the reality he was forced to live with.

"I guess she's doing all right," Nate said. "Fran took me to see her yesterday. And I think she knew who I was this time."

"That's good." From what Bo understood, the woman had been sent to some kind of rehab facility, but there was a question as to what extent she might recover.

"The doctor told us she's doing better," Nate added. "She can feed herself now. I guess that's a good thing."

"Sounds that way to me," Bo said, hoping that was the first of many things she'd be able to accomplish.

Carly's fingers brushed against the cotton fabric of her dress, straightening imaginary wrinkles, which made Bo figure the conversation had tugged on her heartstrings, too.

He had the strongest urge to take her hand and give it a comforting squeeze. But he knew better than that. The kiss they'd shared had connected them in a way neither had been prepared for. And he didn't want to do anything that might strengthen that bond, anything that suggested they'd become a couple.

Or that there would be more tongue-swapping, blood-stirring kisses in their future.

Deciding they were all ready for a change of subject, Bo added, "I hope you're hungry, because my mom is a great cook. Heck, she can throw a beat-up old work boot into a bucket of water, bring it to a boil and make it taste good. Believe me. You're going to come away from her table stuffed to the gills."

"Fran's a pretty good cook, too," Nate said.

Bo was glad to hear it. The poor kid deserved a few breaks, and being able to come home to a hot meal and loving arms was a big one.

Again, Carly's knee brushed his, reminding him of her presence and sending a warm shiver through his veins, unbalancing him yet again.

Even though he did his best to ignore it, he couldn't deny the chemistry, the heat.

It wouldn't take much to drive his better judgment over the edge. Maybe just a quiet place where they could be alone, a yearning glance, a stroke of her skin.

Another stolen kiss.

Bo blew out a silent sigh. Thank goodness they wouldn't find any of that this evening.

Moments later, he parked along the curb in front of the modest, three-bedroom house in South Rosewood where he and his brothers had grown up.

He'd made enough money from his carpentry work to help his retired parents buy a different home, and the other boys had been willing to chip in, too. But Pete and Marla Conway were attached to their neighborhood and refused to consider it.

So instead, Bo had helped them remodel the kitchen and bathrooms and add a new patio and spa in the backyard.

He'd never been ashamed of his family or their simple home, and he wasn't now. But Johnston Lane was a far cry from Danbury Way.

"This neighborhood is a lot different from the one you're used to," Bo told Carly, "but I think you'll enjoy yourself, anyway."

Carly was sure she would. "Believe it or not, I grew up on a street like this. And after meeting your family on Saturday night, I've been looking forward to seeing them all again."

It was strange, though. She'd been a nervous wreck before meeting Greg's parents. And she was a bit anxious now—but in a much different way.

There was a black Harley-Davidson motorcycle parked in the drive, next to a white Buick sedan.

"My brother J.J.'s here already. And my dad must be back with Uncle Roy."

Bo exited the pickup, and Carly slid out on his side, past the steering wheel, rather than out Nate's side. If anyone thought it odd, they didn't say anything.

Nate, who continued to carry the brownies, scanned the fresh-mowed crabgrass, as well as the rose garden on the side of the yard. "Nice place."

"Thanks," Bo said.

They walked up a cracked sidewalk lined with marigolds to the front door, which boasted a pale yellow-and-green wreath made of dried flowers.

He was right. The Conway home was a lot different from the expansive houses and professionally landscaped yards on Danbury Way, but it was far better cared for than the rented duplex in which she'd grown up.

Bo rang the bell, but didn't wait to be let in.

As they stepped into a small, cozy living room, the aroma of roasting beef accosted them, and they were greeted by several woofs and then a pouncing white, curly-haired dog.

"Hey, Mopster." Bo greeted the big and obviously happy critter with a rough-and-tumble hug, which merely caused the dog to list to the side and offer an ear for scratching.

"I'll be right there," Marla called from the other room.

As Bo introduced Nate to the oversize pup, Carly scanned the simple but homey furnishings, the worn, brown tweed sofa, the beige recliner, the bowl of potpourri on the coffee table, several candles and small picture frames on the fireplace mantel. Just to the left of the fireplace, an adjoining wall hosted a display of various family photographs.

"Well, look who's here." Roy's voice sounded from the hall as he wheeled himself into the living room. "And who is this young man?"

Bo straightened, then introduced his uncle to Nate.

Roy stretched out a hand in greeting, and Bo nudged the boy, who'd probably never shaken anyone's hand before.

Nate juggled the plate of brownies and complied.

"Nice grip," Roy said. "I'll bet you're a baseball player."

"Yeah, kind of," Nate said. "But mostly I like basketball."

About that time, Marla swept into the room. "Hi, Carly. Oh, my. Those brownies look delicious."

When Bo introduced his mother to Nate, Marla placed a hand on the lad's shoulder. "I'm so glad you came today. Now the boys will have even teams. My husband, Pete, was afraid he'd have to sit out this time."

Nate beamed, obviously appreciating the warm welcome.

"Can I help with anything?" Carly asked.

"Not yet. But if you'll excuse me for a moment, I'll put these brownies in the kitchen."

"Better hide them," Roy said. "I don't want Pete getting into them before I get a chance to eat my fill."

Within moments, the rest of the Conway brood arrived, Pete, Jr. and his wife, Jennifer, followed by Rick. J.J., who'd been watching ESPN in the den, came out to join the family. Greetings and introductions were made, and before Carly knew it, both she and Nate were drawn into the fold.

The Conways were a strictly blue-collar bunch, and for once in her life, Carly felt completely at ease.

Accepted.

And more than happy to drop pretenses.

While the guys argued over who should get the privilege of having Nate on their team, quickly making the boy feel important, Carly realized that Pete and Marla Conway had done a wonderful job as parents. What other explanation could there be for four such handsome and considerate young men?

"Let me put this in the fridge." Jennifer, her long dark hair plaited in a French braid that hung down her back, carried the salad she'd made into the kitchen.

"I'll help make some room," Marla said. "The beer and soda can go out into the ice chest on the patio."

When the men led Nate to the backyard to shoot hoops, Carly wandered over to the photos on the wall, seeking out pictures of Bo as a child.

There was one of all the kids wearing matching flannel pajamas—red-and-green plaid—and sitting around a Christmas tree.

J.J. doing a wheelie on a bike.

One boy, she had no idea who, was dressed as a clown and holding a trick-or-treat sack.

There was a shot of a teenage Bo playing the guitar in a band.

He'd never mentioned being a musician.

How much more had she to learn about the man and his interests, his talents?

She'd scarcely had a chance to study the pictures when the sound of rubber tires rolling over the hardwood floor alerted her to Roy's approach.

"I see you found the rogues' gallery," he said.

Carly turned, smiling at the man who'd found a spot in her heart, too. "There's something special about this family."

"Me," he admitted. "But then again, I'm biased."

"I can't fault you for that." She returned her gaze to the photos. "You can see the love they share, the pride in each other's accomplishments. It's touching."

"Just like any other family."

No. Not *all* of them.

Not like Nate's. Or Rachel's. And certainly not like Carly's own—at least those tumultuous early years.

Rather than dispute the claim, she turned slightly and reached for a framed photograph from the mantel. It was of Pete, Jr. in a football uniform and sporting black smudge marks under his eyes that made him look like a formidable opponent and not at all like the friendly, warmhearted man she'd first met at Mountain View Manor and had greeted again just moments ago.

"That's Petey," Roy said. "He lettered in football, basketball and baseball in high school. And he managed to graduate with one of those snazzy gold tassels the honor students wore."

"I'll bet Pete and Marla were proud of him."

"They were proud of all their boys, but he was the first-born, the first to go off to kindergarten, to play ball." Roy cleared his throat. "And Petey gave the others something to strive for. Especially Bo, who came along right after him. Some kids would have given up when they had to go head to head with the ultimate boy wonder. But Bo always gave it his best shot."

"Bo was the one most like you," she said, reminding the elderly man of what he'd shared with her on Saturday.

"Petey was a jock, a natural born athlete who made it all look easy, whether he was on the football field, the basketball court or the baseball diamond. He also excelled in the classroom, racking up a bedroom wall full of plaques, ribbons and awards."

Carly, more than anyone, realized how difficult it was when your best was never quite good enough. She might not have had an older sibling to compete with, but she'd had to strive for the unattainable ideal her father had expected.

And unlike Bo, when faced with an obedient and academically successful older sister, Shelby hadn't even tried to compete.

In the past, Carly had considered her wild-child sister to be a party girl, a spoiled kid who lacked focus.

But maybe Shelby had avoided the risk of failure by refusing to try.

Family dynamics and motivation could be confusing.

Carly turned to Roy. "I guess Bo had a rough row to hoe."

"Yep. But by pure guts and determination, he managed to snag his own share of respectable stats, news clippings, trophies and academic honors. The wall on his side of the bedroom wasn't bare. In fact, all of the boys racked up plenty of awards. You'll have to let Marla show you the scrapbooks sometime. She made one for each of them."

Carly would love to see Bo's.

"But there's more to life than scoring points and blocking runs," Roy said. "Some of the boys had to learn that the hard way."

"Oh, yeah?" She leaned against the fireplace mantel. "What do you mean?"

"While at Rosewood J.C., Petey took a pretty hard tumble for a wealthy young woman who'd recently dropped out of an Ivy League college. The spoiled little gal set her sights on him and played him along, toying with him to set off her dad, who had a better prospect in mind for a woman of her status."

For some reason, Carly wondered if the man was baiting her. Or if he thought she might be a spoiled little gal zeroing in on Bo for some self-serving motive.

Either way, she wouldn't take the bait. "I'm sure it wasn't Jennifer."

"Nope. Petey eventually got wise and saw through that crap. And he's got Jenny now, who's a keeper. She sees marriage as a partnership, and she's a real team player."

Before Carly could quiz him more—or maybe find out whether Bo had been talking to his uncle about her—Pete, Sr. woke up from his nap and came into the living room.

The handsome man, who was nearing sixty, yawned. "I'm sorry for dozing off and being a lousy host."

"Don't apologize for that," Roy said. "You don't get enough rest during the week. And in case you haven't figured it out yet, you're not as young as you used to be."

"I know." Pete tossed a smile Carly's way. "I'm glad you came."

"Thanks."

He scanned the room. "Where is everyone?"

Roy pointed toward the east. "The boys are shooting hoops in back with Nate, the kid from the center, the one Bo's been trying to reach."

So Bo had been talking to his uncle, the man he obviously loved and respected.

Pete placed a gentle hand on Carly's shoulder. "If you'll excuse me, I'd better get out there."

"Come on," Roy said to Carly. "Let's go watch them play."

She pushed his chair, maneuvering him outside and finding a place where he could sit in the shade and observe the game. Then she took a seat in a lawn chair next to him, and both Marla and Jennifer soon joined them.

The men were in their element, playing hard, ribbing each other with a fun-loving spirit. But it was the way they included Nate that touched Carly's heart and made her glad she'd come. Glad she had the chance to meet them all.

When Marla announced the meal was ready, everyone trooped inside and feasted on juicy prime rib, roasted red potatoes, green beans with almonds and homemade butter horn rolls. Bo hadn't been one bit biased when he'd said his mom was a good cook.

The table discussion went from weather, to J.J.'s new job at the electric company, to Pete's upcoming retirement from the machine shop, and the Camaro in the garage.

The brownies, which were a big hit and a perfect complement to a mouthwatering meal, were wolfed down quickly.

After eating his fill and wiping his mouth with a paper napkin, Roy glanced at his watch. "The series will be on soon."

"You're right," Pete said. "It's on ESPN at three. The United States team from Ohio is going to have to play their best to beat that Japanese team."

It took Carly awhile, but she finally realized they were talking about the Little League World Series. Bo had told her earlier about Roy coaching the South Rosewood all-star team. And she realized just how far their interest went when, much to her surprise, the entire

Conway clan, including Marla, appeared to be up on all the players, as well as the individual stats.

After watching the game on TV and cheering the American boys—all of them about Nate's age—to victory, the Conways called it a day.

After goodbyes were said, Bo, Carly and Nate climbed into his truck and headed home.

"You've got a wonderful family," Carly exclaimed. "I'm so glad you invited me."

"Yeah, they're really cool," Nate agreed. "Thanks for bringing me, too."

"No problem. I like to show them off once in a while. They're good people."

"I'm especially partial to your uncle Roy," Carly said. "He sure is a character."

"Yeah, Roy's great." Bo's voice had grown soft, yet a bit ragged. "I really love that man."

Bo dropped off Nate first, taking time to talk to Fran and introduce her to Carly. Then he drove across town to Danbury Way.

It had been a wonderful day, both heartwarming and special. And Carly wasn't ready for it to end.

"Would you like to come in for a cup of coffee?"

He paused for what seemed like a long time, then shrugged. "Why not?"

Once inside, she turned on the lights, kicked off her shoes, then led him to the kitchen, where she put on a pot of decaf.

"You really had a good time?" he asked, as though he hadn't expected her to.

"Yes, I did." Carly had been surprised and heartened by his family's warm welcome, but as the day slowly drew to a close, and as they headed back to the McMansion, guilt niggled at her.

"But what?" he asked, as if sensing that there was something amiss, inadvertently zeroing in on the secrets she'd always kept hidden, even from Greg.

Especially from Greg.

But Bo was different. More like her. He had humble roots, too.

But he wasn't ashamed of his humble beginnings, the pesky, small voice whispered, resurrecting itself from the place where she'd banished it. *He's proud of his family.*

Just wait one minute, Carly countered. She had a loving mother, too. And a sister who, in spite of the trouble she always seemed to get into, was a kindhearted sort. Maybe too much so when it came to choosing friends and people to trust.

Still, the truth came rushing to the forefront.

Carly had kept her past hidden from her ex-husband, neighbors and friends. And she'd kept her mom and sister at arm's length, too.

Okay, so her mom was a homebody. And probably a bit agoraphobic. But that didn't mean Carly couldn't have taken Greg with her on those visits to Texas.

Bo closed the gap between them, catching her chin with the tip of his finger. "What's the matter?"

"I don't know," she lied.

How pitiful was that?

She cleared her throat, wondering where a bit of honesty would get her. And then wondering whether Bo would be as understanding as he'd always been if she unloaded the burden she'd carried alone for years.

"I guess I'm just a bit envious," she admitted. "That's all."

His hand slipped to her shoulder, his musky scent settling over her. "About what?"

"The closeness your family shares. The bond. The support."

"You didn't have that growing up?"

No.

Well, that wasn't exactly true. She, her mom and sister had shared a closeness. An alliance, she supposed. But after her father had left, she'd failed to cultivate the bond. Failed to hold on to it.

Instead of resorting to the background she'd fabricated, as she'd done each time Greg had broached the subject, she merely downplayed the truth.

"My growing up years were okay. I really have nothing to complain about. There's just something special that radiates around you and your family. Something that fills the house with joy."

"It's love," he said.

"I know." It was what she desperately wanted for herself and Bo.

Their gazes locked, and emotion swirled, charged and complicated, yet as subtle as a dream come true.

She decided to step out farther on a limb, much like Rachel did each day on the playground. One foot in front of the other. Not looking at where she'd been or where she was, but on where she wanted to go.

"Do you feel what's happening between us?"

He nodded. "Yeah. I feel it. But I'm not sure what to do about it."

Sometimes a person had to take a chance. To risk it all for the dream. And in Carly's case, that dream was love.

"I know what to do about it," she said.

Then she slipped her arms around his neck and raised her lips to his.

Chapter Twelve

For a guy who hated to lose, Bo gave up the long, grueling struggle the moment Carly pressed her sweet mouth to his.

She'd shown her mettle and an awesome ability to not only charm his family, but to be charmed as well.

There were probably a hundred arguments he could offer himself, but not a single one that could convince him he didn't want this, didn't want her.

The kiss deepened, and their tongues dipped and twisted, tasting, seeking. Their hands groped, grasped, caressed.

He relished the feel of her breasts pressed against his chest, of her heart beating against his. He'd give anything to carry her to bed, to claim her as his own and make love with her all night long. But he wouldn't think that far ahead, wouldn't let himself do anything but enjoy the moment.

As the kiss deepened, as their breaths mingled, Carly whimpered and leaned into him, pressing against his erection, making her need clear and intensifying his own.

Raw heat damn near exploded.

He'd never been so fully aroused, so filled with desire.

She broke the kiss just long enough to nuzzle his cheek and whisper, "I want to make love, Bo. Stay with me tonight."

And then what? he wanted to ask.

Would they both be sated? Ready to call it quits and get on with their own lives, no one being the wiser?

But reason flew out the window, and passion took over. All he could think of was taking Carly to bed and removing their clothes. Making love until dawn and waking in each other's arms.

He took her face in his hands, his palms against her jaw, his thumbs brushing the silk of her cheeks. His gaze zeroed in on hers, spotting the heat, the longing. "We might be sorry in the morning."

"I doubt it. And so do you."

She was right. And he couldn't bring himself to pretend otherwise.

"I want you, Carly. More than I ought to."

She smiled, then grasped his hand and led him to the staircase.

When they reached the landing, they strode down the

hall, but as they approached the master bedroom, he balked and drew her back. "Not in there."

She nodded, as though sensing his need to break free of Greg, of his memory.

Bo might have always enjoyed competing with his older brother, sometimes winning, sometimes coming in a close second. And failure had never sat well with him. But he'd never feared it. Never worried that he couldn't live up to his parents' expectations, which had never been more than he could achieve.

He'd always been loved, accepted for himself.

But this was different.

Opening himself and his feelings to Carly made him more vulnerable than he'd ever been.

Still, the desire to finish what they'd started, to feel her body against his—skin to skin and heart to heart—was overwhelming.

She led him to a guest room, one of many, then slowly closed the door. As she turned and presented her back, she lifted her hair to make it easy for him to unzip her dress. And he shoved her ex from his mind, refusing to think of anything but the need to bury himself deep within her, to love her with all he had to give, to be one with her tonight.

His fingers actually fumbled, but not in nervousness. In awe and wonder.

Like a kid who'd been given a pile of Christmas presents in August, he slipped the sides of her dress over her shoulders and pressed a kiss against her neck, savoring the satin of her skin and her spring-garden scent.

She slowly turned to face him, then peeled off the fabric the rest of the way and let it fall to the floor. As she stood before him in a lacy white bra and matching thong, his breath caught at the beauty of her, at the gift she offered.

"Aw, Carly." His voice was raw with need, with yearning. With desire. "I don't deserve you."

"Yes you do."

Carly had never known love could be like this, so open. So real. She tugged Bo's shirt from the waistband of his jeans, then he helped her remove it. She ran her fingers over his broad chest, over the well-defined abs—toned by an honest day's work, tanned by the summer sun.

She'd never wanted a man more, never needed one more. She wrapped her arms around him, felt his skin against her breasts. Her nipples tingled and hardened.

He kissed her long and thoroughly, taking his time until she was wild with need.

She tugged at his belt, letting him know she was ready for more, ready for him.

Then he placed his hand over hers.

"What's the matter?" she asked, hoping he wasn't having a change of heart.

"I don't have any condoms with me."

"That's all right. I'm on the pill." She expected him to be grateful, to be glad they didn't have to worry about pausing to mess with latex or to worry about pregnancy.

But he seemed to sober.

"What's wrong?"

Bo didn't know what to say, how to tell her that he was knotted up inside.

There'd only been one reason for her to remain on the pill after Greg had left. She was expecting her husband to come back. And she wanted to be ready for him when he did.

"Are you sure about this?" he asked, raking a hand through his hair.

"Yes." She placed her palms on his chest, the caress of her fingers sending a rush of heat through his veins. "I'm sure. More than I've ever been."

The coward told him it wouldn't be worth the risk. That making love would only make him fall deeper in love with another man's wife.

Yeah. The divorce was final. But did love completely die? And if it did, could it be resurrected?

He struggled with fear and guilt, as well as the desire to take what she was clearly offering, even if it was just for this night.

But lust won out. That and the need to taste her again, to give her all he had to give, then hold her during the afterglow, to stay until dawn and wake in her arms.

Yielding to temptation, he placed a kiss on her brow. "I hope we aren't sorry about this tomorrow."

"We won't be."

He planned to do his damnedest to make sure *she* wasn't. But that didn't mean he could do anything to protect himself.

Sweeping her into his arms, he carried her to the

bed. And after undressing, he joined her, taking his time to love her with his caresses, with his kisses.

And she did the same.

When they were so caught up in raging desire that they reached a point of now or never, he hovered over her, and she opened for him, placing her hands on his hips, as though guiding him home.

Where he belonged.

He entered her, and as she arched to meet him, she took all he had to offer, sharing all she had in return.

As they peaked, Carly clutched his shoulders. And when she climaxed, her nails dug into his back. She cried out in pleasure, just as he found his own release in a neck-arching, mind-soaring burst of color.

Holding her until the last throbbing wave of their orgasms had ended, he remained on top, afraid to move, afraid to speak.

"I had no idea," she finally said.

Neither had he.

"It was better than I'd imagined."

What was that supposed to mean? That she'd been dreaming of what it might be like with him?

Or that she hadn't expected all that much?

Damn. He hated the insecurity. He'd never had to deal with it before. Especially when it came to sex.

He rolled to the side, taking her with him.

He brushed a strand of hair from her eyes, yet continued to hold her close, to relish her scent, the feel of her sweet body in his arms. "Not bad for our first time."

"You mean it's only going to get better?" She blessed him with a heartwarming smile.

"That's hard for me to imagine," he admitted. "But it's early yet."

As the sun peered through a crack in the wood shutters, Carly closed her eyes and basked in the warmth of Bo's embrace.

Making love had been far better than she'd ever imagined it to be. And she wasn't just talking about those fantasies she'd been having since she and Bo had kissed that very first time.

She was talking about all those magazine articles she'd read, the ones that had suggested she and Greg had been missing something.

Whew.

Now she knew the articles had been right. And she suspected that even the writers of those articles had missed out on something in their sexual relationships, too.

Bo had said it was early yet. And it was.

They hadn't discussed the future. But she knew exactly what she wanted—to remain in Bo's arms, wrapped in his love, forever.

Okay. So they hadn't mentioned love. Not directly. But they'd tiptoed around it.

There was no doubt in her mind of what she was feeling. It was love through and through. And whatever she'd felt for Greg paled in comparison.

Bo's arms drew her closer, and she realized he was waking again.

She glanced at the alarm clock on the nightstand. It was nearly eleven, and she'd slept later than she had in ages. But she shouldn't be surprised. She'd never made love until dawn before, never felt so pleasantly exhausted and completely sated.

A grin tugged at her lips, and she turned in her lover's arms, facing him. Catching the glimmer in his eye, realizing he'd enjoyed their night together, too.

"Good morning," she whispered.

"Same to you." He ran a hand possessively along her hip. "I wondered what you looked like in the morning."

She stiffened, suddenly thinking about morning breath, dried sleep in her eyes, smudged mascara....

He brushed a kiss across her lips. "I can't believe all that time you must have spent applying makeup, styling your hair. And it wasn't necessary. You look so much better to me like this."

She grinned. "You mean completely spent following a night of back-to-back orgasms?"

"Sexual satisfaction looks especially nice on you. And it makes me want to beat my chest with my fists and roar."

She was the one who ought to boast. She couldn't believe her luck, her good fortune. Bo was not only an incredible lover, but he'd also become her best friend.

"You know what?" she asked without waiting for his response. "I can be myself with you. And that's something I've never been able to do with anyone else."

"I'm glad. I don't want there to be any secrets between us."

She didn't want there to be, either.

But there was one.

One she'd been afraid to tell Greg. One she hadn't trusted him enough to reveal.

Yet Bo was different. He'd always been accepting of her. If she could entrust her heart or her secrets with anyone, it would be him. And if they were going to have the kind of loving, lifelong commitment Roy had talked about, there shouldn't be any secrets between them.

"I want to tell you something," she said, hoping that she had the guts to press on.

"What's that?"

There was still time to change course, to sidestep the past.

"I, uh, really enjoyed being with your family last night." She wasn't sure whether she was fishing for an opening or falling back on old habits.

"I'm glad. They liked having you there, too."

"They're great people."

He didn't respond, didn't need to.

She could still veer off subject and let the whole thing drop. But hanging on to her secret and guilt would mar the sweet moment they were sharing, and shadow the future she hoped they'd have together.

"I told you that I grew up in a home much like yours," she said. "But that's not entirely true. My early years were filled with criticism and resentment. Not love and acceptance."

He brushed a strand of hair from her eyes. "I'm sorry to hear that."

She believed he was, and forced herself to continue. "I grew up in a run-down duplex on the outskirts of Milburn Flats, Texas." She closed her eyes, digging deep into her memory, hoping that by uncovering her secrets, she would be able to fully relish all she and Bo had shared last night. The intimacy. The closeness.

The promise of a bright future together.

So she continued. "My dad was a retired drill instructor and a long-haul trucker. He was away from home more often than not, but whenever he was around, he used to browbeat my mom, my sister and me."

Bo continued to hold her, to offer his silent support.

"He used to tear into my mom something awful. And whenever he left on a run, she'd fill her evenings eating potato chips, peanut butter cookies and fudge ripple ice cream. As a result, she put on a lot of weight—enough to eventually play havoc with her knees and health.

"It didn't take long for my sister and me to fall into the same pattern. According to my dad, I was homely and too fat. And by the time I reached my teen years, I struggled with a ton of self-esteem issues."

"I'm sorry you had to go through that," Bo said. "And I'm surprised that a glance in the mirror couldn't put those unfounded worries to rest."

"Believe me, I tried that. But all I saw was a crooked nose, a chipped front tooth and broad hips."

"Your dad was a jerk, Carly."

"Yes, he was. Fortunately, when I was a sophomore in high school, he left on a cross-country trip and never returned. Later, we found out that he'd fallen for a waitress in another state and had decided to create a new family with her."

"His desertion sounds to me like a blessing."

"It was. And even though my mom had to work two jobs to support us, we were a lot better off." Carly shrugged again. "Maybe I was the only one who came out on top. My sister became bulimic and spent too much time looking for love in all the wrong places."

"I'm glad you didn't let it get to you," he said. "Not to that point, anyway."

"I poured myself into my studies, received a scholarship and went to college, where I managed to drop about twenty or thirty pounds and start a self-improvement crusade. I met Greg, fell in love and got married. You know the rest. About me, anyway."

"What about your mom and sister?"

"They still live in Texas. When Greg and I became engaged, Shelby was seventeen and announced that she was not only pregnant, but didn't have a clue who the father of her baby was." Carly took a deep breath, then slowly blew it out, hoping to release all she'd been hiding, all she'd been holding back. Not just the truth about the past, but the resentment and the guilt she'd suffered because of it.

"Did your sister keep the baby?" he asked. "Do you have a niece or nephew?"

"Actually, Shelby miscarried the day she and my mom were supposed to have flown out to the wedding. They both missed it, of course."

Her mind drifted to the day she'd walked down the aisle, escorted by a man she'd just met, a friend of Greg's father.

She'd still felt very much alone and out of her element. "The entire church was filled to capacity, and the only two family members I had were noticeably absent."

"I'm sorry. That must have been disappointing to have them miss your big day."

"It was. But in a way, I was also relieved. And I've had to live with that, too. The conflicting emotion, I mean. I was hurt that they weren't there and angry that Shelby managed to screw up again, even if she hadn't meant to. And I was a bit envious that my mom chose Shelby over me. *Again.* Yet at the same time I knew why she would, and I felt like a spoiled brat for not being more sympathetic about what Shelby was going through." Carly blew out a weary sigh. "How pitiful is that?"

"It's not the least bit pitiful. And I don't think you should beat yourself up about it."

No?

He ran his knuckles along her cheek. "I can understand why you'd feel conflicting emotions."

"You can?" She'd hoped he would, and it made it easier to continue to lay it all on the line. "I went to visit my mom and sister in Texas yearly, but I made the reservations when I knew things were especially busy for Greg at work. I never wanted him to know that I was embarrassed by their living conditions, by some of the stupid things my sister would do and the losers she would get involved with."

"So what are you really struggling with?" Bo asked, as though he could see right through her.

But he had all along, hadn't he?

"It's not like I've forgotten about them completely," she said. "I've been sending my mom money each month. And I call regularly."

"But you feel guilty," Bo stated.

"Yes. And seeing your family last night only made me realize that I'd let mine down. That I should be doing more. That I ought to go out to see them again. And maybe I should even invite Shelby to come out here, to stay with me so that I can introduce her to different people and show her a new life."

"Sounds like a good idea, one that might do you all a bit of good." Bo pressed a kiss on the tip Carly's nose. "I'm sure you'll do the right thing."

The right thing.

Interestingly enough, since she and Bo had become friends, she was doing all the right things: forgetting about the obsession to be more than she really was; volunteering to help those who weren't as fortunate as her; being honest with the man she was growing to love more each day.

"Thanks, Bo. You have no idea how good it feels to have someone in my corner, someone who understands."

"Didn't Greg offer you any support? Didn't he encourage you to have a relationship with your family?"

"No."

"That surprises me," Bo said.

"It's really not his fault," she confessed. "In retrospect, maybe he would have, if I'd told him the truth about my past and shared my feelings."

Would Bo understand why she hadn't been able to open up with Greg? And that she felt safe enough wrapped in Bo's arms to be able to share it with him instead?

Her gaze connected with his, and she placed a hand on his cheek, felt the bristle he would shave later this morning.

Love swelled in her heart, filling it in a way it had never been filled. She'd hinted at it before. But now that she was feeling secure and strong, she would let him know exactly what it was she was feeling. No more secrets. No more swallowed emotions.

"I love you, Bo."

Her words slammed into Bo's chest.

Carly loved him?

More than anything in the world he wanted to believe her. Wanted to take a chance and risk it all.

But before he could respond to her admission of love, the phone rang.

"You'd better get that," he said, wanting more time

to decide whether he should admit that he'd fallen in love with her, too.

Carly rolled over and snatched the telephone from the nightstand. "Hello?"

As she listened to the person on the other end, she pulled the sheets to her chest, covering herself. "Hi."

Her expression flickered, as though a hundred thoughts were crossing her mind, and she tucked a strand of hair behind her ear. "Sure. I'll meet you."

She paled, then sat up in bed, still clutching the sheet and drawing it closer. Her grip tightened on the receiver until her knuckles whitened. "You have to be kidding. *Now?*"

Bo propped himself up on an elbow, wondering what in the hell was going on. He tapped her on the shoulder, and when she turned, he furrowed his brow and mouthed, "Who is it?"

She covered the phone with her hand and whispered, "Greg."

Bo's heart sunk to the pit of his stomach, yet he nodded as though the call had been expected, as though it was only natural that Greg would want to speak to the woman he'd married, the woman he'd vowed to love until death parted them.

Like a robot, Bo climbed out of bed and reached for his pants. It would have been so much better if Greg had called yesterday, before Bo and Carly had made love.

Yet the ache in his chest suggested it would have been even better if the call had never come at all.

Either way, Greg's timing sucked.

Chapter Thirteen

"Greg wants to talk to me," Carly admitted after hanging up the phone.

"What about?"

"I don't know. But he says it's important."

"Are you going to meet him someplace?"

"He's on his way *here*."

Bo tried to appear unruffled, but wasn't sure if he could pull it off. "Maybe I'd better go."

"That's not necessary."

It felt necessary to Bo. "It's probably best if my truck isn't in your driveway when he arrives."

"I don't care if he sees it. But even if I did, you don't have time to move it. He's just down the street." She went to her room across the hall, then returned with a white silk robe and slipped it on to cover her naked body.

"I'll just leave," Bo told her, zipping his pants and reaching for the shirt that had ended up on the floor last night. "It'll give you two a chance to talk in private."

"No. Wait here. I have a feeling we'll need to talk after he goes."

So did Bo.

As she fussed with the sash of her robe, Bo studied her.

There wasn't much between her body and a man's eye. Just a veil of silk. Apparently she didn't have time to shower, but he wondered why she didn't throw on some clothes. Something that would cover her more.

But then again, it wasn't as if Greg hadn't seen her naked before.

Damn.

Bo didn't like this situation. Not one bit.

He wondered if she was going to comb her hair, maybe put on some lipstick or something. After all, she'd always wanted to look her best for Greg.

To be her best.

"Tell me something," he said. "Why didn't you ever tell Greg about your past, about how bad things were for you while you were a kid?"

"I probably should have," she said. "But his mother was so critical about what was proper, what was expected, that I was afraid he'd be ashamed of me."

She used her fingers to comb through her hair, but

didn't glance in the mirror. "I wanted him to see me as perfect."

"It's the flaws that make a person real. And it's honesty that makes a relationship special."

"Yes," she said. "I can see that now. Looking back, I probably should have been honest with him from day one. Then he wouldn't have complained that I was holding something back, that there was a part of me I wouldn't share with him."

And maybe Greg wouldn't have left her.

The words hadn't been spoken, but the message came through loud and clear.

The doorbell rang—a formal gong resonating throughout the house, announcing the end of what they'd shared last night.

All that Bo believed about marriages, about husbands and wives, about commitments, came back to haunt him now.

How could he stand in the way of something that was meant to be? Of solemn vows made a long time ago?

"You have to tell him, Carly. He deserves to know."

She stiffened, and her fingers fiddled with the edge of her sash.

The part of him that believed second place wasn't good enough, especially in a relationship with Carly, battled his sense of ethics when it came to love and marriage. "I'm going to take a shower and allow you some privacy. But don't feel as though you owe me anything. We didn't make any promises."

The doorbell rang again, insistently. And Carly seemed to grow even more pale.

"Go," he told her. "And be honest with him."

She reached for Bo's hand, giving it a squeeze with fingers that were cool to the touch. "Wait for me in here. I won't be long."

He wasn't so sure about that. But when she did come back, if she was pondering any kind of a decision between the two of them, he wasn't sure what he'd do. He'd never feared losing before. He just hadn't liked it.

But this was different.

Maybe he ought to make it easy on her and let her go without a fight, even if it damn near killed him.

And as he headed for the shower, he feared that it might.

If Carly didn't know better, she'd think Bo was pushing her away, withdrawing.

As she reached the foyer, she hesitated, wanting to turn back to him and make her heart and her choice known. But he'd been right.

She owed it to Greg to tell him the truth about everything. Even the checks she'd sent monthly to her mother for the entire seven years of their marriage. So she opened the door, apologizing for being slow to answer, but not for her appearance. After all, Greg had been unexpected.

And uninvited.

The man who'd once been her husband looked the same—tall and handsome, with an athletic build. His brown hair was neatly styled. But the attraction she'd once felt had faded noticeably.

"I really didn't mean to intrude," he said. "But there's something that needs to be said, and I'm glad I finally found you at home."

"You've driven by the house?"

"A couple of times. And I called before, but didn't leave a message. I thought it would be best to meet face-to-face."

"Do you want to come in?"

"If you don't mind."

She nodded, then led him into the den and closed the door.

He took a seat on the sofa, next to the armrest. "Megan encouraged me to come and talk to you."

Carly stiffened. "Why?"

"She thought you and I needed to talk about a few things."

"Such as...?"

"We need closure, especially if we're going to live in the same neighborhood."

Carly was up for some closure, even if she wasn't sure she wanted to remain living in the McMansion. That was something she'd decide later, after talking to Bo.

"Megan's probably right," she admitted. "I have something to say, too. Things I should have revealed years ago."

Starting at the beginning, she told him about the home she'd grown up in, about the man who'd belittled her. She went on to share that her mother had gotten heavy and was suffering health problems, and that her sister had an eating disorder and had made some lousy choices over the years.

Greg listened intently, never once indicating judgment.

"When we met in college," she told him, "you represented the life I'd never had, a way out." She tugged at her robe, wishing she'd taken the time to dress, but realizing she'd feel naked, anyway. She blew out a sigh. "I did love you, Greg. But I was so insecure. I was afraid that if you saw my flaws or those of my family, you'd find me lacking and leave. So I tried my best to be the perfect wife, to make a perfect home for you."

"And the harder you tried, the more you shut me out." Greg leaned back into the cushions of the sofa, propped his elbow on the armrest. "Whenever I tried to get you to open up, you brushed me off. I thought if I indulged your decorating projects it would make you happy. Maybe it did, but something was always wrong."

"I created a new past for myself," she admitted. "And I kept the real one a secret. And because of that, I lost out on having a better relationship with my mother and sister."

"You could have flown them out here. Or gone to see them as often as you liked. I wouldn't have minded."

"I realize that. *Now,* anyway."

Revealing the truth to Greg, even though it was about eight years too late, removed the bonds that had imprisoned her. It also strengthened her, building her self-confidence even further.

"There's one more thing I should have told you. Something I've felt guilty about."

"What's that?"

"My mom has been on disability and struggling to make ends meet. And I apologize for not running this by you first, but I used to send her a couple of hundred dollars each month out of my household allowance."

"You're right," he said. "You should have told me. Believe it or not, I would have encouraged you to send her more."

Tears welled in Carly's eyes, and a drop slid down her cheek, followed by another. "You're a great guy, Greg. I'm sorry that I didn't fully appreciate your kindness or your generosity."

"Yeah, well, I'm sorry you didn't feel secure enough in our marriage to be honest with me."

"It wasn't you," she admitted. "It was me. My fears. My hang-ups."

"It's a shame. In all the years we spent together, we never really fought, but we never had a *real* relationship, either."

She knew that now. And she suspected that's what he'd finally found with Megan. Something real.

"Are you happy?" she asked.

"Yes, life is good. But I didn't mean for my happiness to be at your expense. I never wanted to hurt you."

"I'm sure you didn't. But looking back, I think it was more my pride than my heart that was wounded."

And there was a reason for that. She'd been in such

a hurry to marry, to secure a happy future and a loving home of her own, that it had never occurred to her Greg might not be the right man for her. "I think I was more in love with the idea of being married."

"I hope things work out for you," he said. "And that you'll find the happiness you deserve."

She cast him a smile. "We've both moved on, Greg. And it's all for the best."

Eager to get back upstairs and talk to Bo, to tell him that her love for him was real and that loving him made her a better person, she stood.

Greg got to his feet as well. "There's just one more thing."

"What's that?"

"Please don't blame Megan for any of our problems. There was never anything between us until after the divorce was final. Not a smile, not a glance. And when our paths crossed, I did the pursuing. Not Megan."

It had been that way between Carly and Bo, too. He'd been a perfect gentleman. And she'd been the one to pursue him.

"I believe you, Greg. Thanks for stopping by."

He nodded, then headed for the door.

She watched him leave, realizing that she'd taken control of her own life for the first time in years.

And maybe for the first time ever.

As she turned and placed her hand on the banister, preparing to climb the stairs and return to Bo, she paused.

There was something else she needed to do before talking to Bo about what the future might hold for them.

"Where the hell is she?" Bo muttered to himself as he paced the floor in the guest room where they'd slept, where the sheets still carried the scent of their lovemaking, reminding him of what he and Carly had shared.

Of all he stood to lose.

Lose. He chuffed at the sting of defeat, hating the feeling he'd never gotten used to. The thought of losing Carly to Greg was tearing him up inside.

He glanced at the alarm clock. What was keeping her? He'd already taken a shower. A long one. Then he'd gotten dressed.

Damn. What could they be talking about? What were they doing?

He didn't like Carly and Greg being together this long. Didn't like it at all. The more time they spent together, the more apparent it was that they were mending fences, settling differences.

What luck, huh?

Just when he'd realized he'd fallen head over heart in love, just when he'd had a glimpse of forever, the portal was closing before his eyes.

He'd told himself he should bow out graciously when she returned, but that was a crock. He might ultimately lose Carly to Greg, but Bo couldn't just stand there and let her go without a fight, even if it was merely a revelation of what she meant to him.

Bracing for the worst, yet determined to face the conflict head-on, he strode down the hall toward the stairs.

When he reached the living room, he found it empty.

Next he went to the kitchen, then to the formal dining room.

Where the hell were they? Outside? Standing on the front porch?

In the foyer, he spotted the closed door to the den out of the corner of his eye.

And as he drew near, he heard a muffled voice inside.

Damn.

Unable to help himself, he knocked lightly. Then louder. "Carly?"

"Come in," she said.

He was almost afraid to, but it was better than rolling over and giving her up. So he opened the door, only to find Carly alone and talking on the telephone.

Embarrassed and feeling foolish, he started to back away.

"Wait, Bo." She covered the mouthpiece. "This is my mom. I'm flying home to visit her and my sister in two weeks. And if you can take some time off, I'd like you to go with me."

Him?

She wanted *him* to go with her, not Greg?

"Listen, Mom," she said, a smile bursting out on her face. "I have to go. But I'm thrilled that the new weight loss program is working so well. And I'll call you tomorrow night. I'd like to hear what the doctor has to say when you see him in the morning. A forty-three pound loss is great. I'll bet your cholesterol is better, too."

When she disconnected, Carly turned to him, beaming. "You were right, Bo. In fact, it felt so good to level with Greg and to find some closure that I had to call my mom and finally tell her about the divorce. To let her know that I'm okay with it."

"Was she upset?"

"Yes. At first. But when I explained that I'd been just as unhappy as Greg had been, and that I've finally met the right man, she felt better."

"You've met the right man?" Bo asked, wanting to hear her say it all again. That she loved him.

She nodded, her smile broadening and continuing to light her face. "First I had to find myself, though." She scooted her chair away from the desk, stood and walked toward him. "And once I did, I realized it was okay to fall short of perfection. And that the right man wouldn't leave me just because I'm human."

A grin tugged at his lips. "Oh, yeah? Why don't you tell me about that man. The one you told your mother you'd found."

She stepped into his embrace and slipped her arms around his neck. "I knew you were a talented carpenter. I've seen you work wonders with wood and plaster. But little did I know you'd work that same magic on me, starting at the very foundation, at the very heart of me. I love you, Bo."

"I love you, too, honey. More than I'd ever imagined

I could love anyone." He drew her close, held her tight. Then he kissed her. Softly at first—reverently, then deeper, hinting at the promise of a future filled with love and all that was right with the world.

When the kiss ended, as she stepped out of his embrace, she fiddled with the lapel of her robe, then combed her fingers through the messy strands of her hair. "I'd better take a shower. I probably look a fright. And how pitif—"

She stopped herself. "It's not pitiful, is it?"

"Not one bit." He kissed her brow. "You look as though you spent the night in my arms, taking me places I'd never been."

"I'm glad. But I still need to jump in the shower."

He hoped she wasn't planning to do so alone. "Maybe I ought to take another one, too."

Joy splashed across her face. "I don't suppose you'd be interested in conserving water."

"No," he said, "I have a feeling we're going to waste some. But let's only mess up one bathroom."

Carly took him by the hand and led him toward the stairs. "I know we have plenty of things to discuss. Maybe we can set aside some time for that later this afternoon."

"What kind of things do you want to talk about?" he asked, as they reached the guest room where they'd touched the moon and stars last night.

"Like whether you can go to Texas with me. And whether you'd mind if I applied to be a foster mother. I'd like to offer Rachel a home."

"Yes and no."

She tugged at his hand, stopping him. "You have reservations about going to Texas and me being a foster mother to Rachel?"

"Yes, I'll go to Texas, assuming I have time to work my schedule around it. And no, I don't have a problem with you parenting Rachel. You'll make a great mother. To her, or to any children we might have."

Carly smiled, pleased to have his love and support. "I'd also like to go back to college and get a degree. It's important for me to do that."

"That means it's important to me, too."

They sealed their love with a kiss, one that promised the moon and offered them a glimpse of heaven.

Life didn't get any more perfect than that.

* * * * *

Workaholic Molly Jackson can handle absolutely *anything*—except an unexpected pregnancy! But when her best friend, Adam, talks her into a marriage of convenience for the baby's sake, sparks of romance shock her even more....

Look for the next book in the new
Special Edition continuity,
TALK OF THE NEIGHBOURHOOD,
A Little Change of Plans *by Jen Safrey.*
On sale September 2007 wherever
Mills & Boon books are sold.

Sierra's Homecoming

by

Linda Lael Miller

Soft, smoky music poured into the room.

The next thing she knew, Sierra was in Travis's arms, close against that chest she'd admired earlier, and they were slow dancing.

Why didn't she pull away?

"Relax," he said. His breath was warm in her hair.

She giggled, more nervous than amused. What was the matter with her? She was attracted to Travis, had been from the first, and he was clearly attracted to her. They were both adults. Why not enjoy a little slow dancing in a ranch-house kitchen?

Because slow dancing led to other things. She took a step back and felt the counter flush against her lower back. Travis naturally came with her, since they were holding hands and he had one arm around her waist.

Simple physics.

Then he kissed her.

Physics again—this time, not so simple.

"Yikes," she said, when their mouths parted.

He grinned. "Nobody's ever said that after I kissed them."

She felt the heat and substance of his body pressed against hers. "It's going to happen, isn't it?" she heard herself whisper.

"Yep," Travis answered.

"But not tonight," Sierra said on a sigh.

"Probably not," Travis agreed.

"When, then?"

He chuckled, gave her a slow, nibbling kiss. "Tomorrow morning," he said. "After you drop Liam off at school."

"Isn't that…a little…soon?"

"Not soon enough," Travis answered, his voice husky. "Not nearly soon enough."

* * * *

Don't forget Sierra's Homecoming *is a December novel.*

Special
moments

We hope that the Special Edition novel you have just
finished has given you plenty of romantic
reading pleasure.

We are thrilled to have put together a section of
special free bonus features, which we hope will add to
the entertainment in each Special Edition novel from
now on.

There will be puzzles for you to do, exciting
horoscopes glimpsing what's in your future, author
information and sneak previews of books in
the pipeline!

Do let us know what you think of these
special extras by emailing
specialmoments@hmb.co.uk

For you, from us…
Relax and enjoy…

★ **fun** Star *signs*
puzzles

Judy *Duarte*

Dear Reader,

When my editor asked me to write book two in *TALK OF THE NEIGHBOURHOOD*, I loved the idea of a series based upon the neighbours of Danbury Way. And I was especially pleased to create Carly's story, since I'd gone through an unexpected divorce, too.

As someone who tried to make everyone happy – sometimes at my own expense – it was difficult to realise I couldn't fix things, no matter how hard I tried. Yet the months passed, and the lessons I learned along the way made me a better, stronger person.

And you know what? It was all worth it in the long run, because I met my very own hero, a man who loved me enough to take on the responsibility of four children.

No, I'm not a perfect wife. And it's been ages since I was a size ten, but I've learned to be myself and not someone others expect me to be.

I hope you enjoy reading about Carly's journey in *The Perfect Wife*. And I wish you all a happy-ever-after.

Love,
Judy

Special
moments

JUDY DUARTE

An avid reader who enjoys a happy ending, Judy Duarte loves to create stories of her own. When she's not cooped up in her writing cave, she's spending time with her somewhat enormous, but delightfully close, family.

Judy makes her home in California with her personal hero, their youngest son and a cat named Mum. "Sharing a name with the family pet gets a bit confusing," she admits. "Especially when the cat decides to curl up in a secluded cubbyhole and hide. I'm not sure what the neighbours think when my son walks up and down the street calling for Mum."

You can write to Judy c/o Silhouette Books, 233 Broadway, Suite 1001, New York, NY 10279, USA. Or you can contact her through her website at: www.judyduarte.com.

Phraseology

Copyright ©2006 PuzzleJunction.com

5 letter words

E-mail

Gum up

No one

No-win

6 letter words

Eat out

Give in

Go awry

Jet lag

Keep up

Mud pie

Pass on

Stop by

Too big

7 letter words

Equal to

Net loss

Old maid

Rag doll

Take aim

Tried on

8 letter words

Drags out

Ewe-lambs

Merry men

What next

9 letter words

Get in line

Votes down

Special *moments*

Sud*oku*

To solve the Sudoku puzzle, each row, column and
box must contain the numbers 1 to 9.

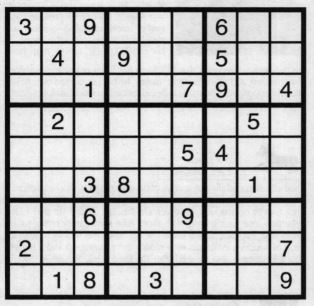

3		9				6		
	4		9			5		
		1			7	9		4
	2						5	
					5	4		
		3	8				1	
		6			9			
2								7
	1	8		3				9

Horoscopes

Dadhichi is a renowned astrologer and is frequently seen on TV and in the media. He has the unique ability to draw from complex astrological theory to provide clear, easily understandable advice and insights for people who want to know what their future may hold.

In the twenty-five years that Dadhichi has been practising astrology, face reading and other esoteric studies, he has conducted over 8,500 consultations. His clients include celebrities, political and diplomatic figures and media and corporate identities from all over the world.

Aries
21 March - 20 April

You can successfully bring your plans and projects to completion this month. You need to control your nerves and also your reaction to co-workers, however. On the 1st, 2nd, 14th and 15th, you may lose your temper with those who are actually trying to help you. Patience seems to be the key word this month to assure you of success. Problems with money are clearing up and a better bank balance is also assured after the third week of August.

Taurus
21 April - 21 May

Unusual people will be part of your life this month and your popularity will be strong when you least expect it. You'll seem to be more in demand and this has everything to do with your forceful and vibrant personality. Between the 4th and the 10th you'll be riding the wave of social popularity. Enjoy it as much as you can.

Special *moments*

by *Dadhichi Toth*

Gemini
22 May - 22 June

Although your work seems set to reach a new plateau, you mustn't let your health or that of someone else become an obstacle to greater achievements. On the 6th and the 14th, listen to your body signals and have that check-up to reduce your worry, if nothing else. A friend will invite you to travel, but your work commitments may not allow you the freedom you would like.

Cancer
23 June - 23 July

Positive news from someone at a distance will amuse and lift your spirits. After the 5th, your communications with others will be cordial, if not humorous. Practical jokes and novel circumstances break the tedium of day-to-day life. Friends' problems will be greatly relieved by your own sense of humour. An opportunity is presented by a rival or opposition company and is worth considering.

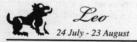

Leo
24 July - 23 August

Many happy returns, Leo! The Sun will revitalise your personality and all your relationships during the coming three or four weeks. Although greater responsibilities are indicated from the 12th, your happy disposition is likely to meet these challenges with a can-do attitude. Money or valuables that are suddenly lost will reappear just as mysteriously.

Virgo
24 August - 22 September

Sudden infatuations are likely to excite but also confuse you, as others won't show their hand. Honesty will be necessary to keep you on the right track. Your service-orientated personality will be called upon to assist people in dire straits, especially after the 10th. Playing the compassionate game to genuine people is commendable, but you need to sift the wheat from the chaff. Don't be a sucker for a hard-luck story.

Libra
23 September - 23 October

Extra debts make the first week of August difficult for you. You have to work hard to overcome worries and use your creativity to dig yourself out of a financial ditch. Discussions with bank managers on the 4th and the 6th will work magic and restore your confidence. Collaborative interviews with employers are also set to change the complexion of your work after the 17th.

Scorpio
24 October - 22 November

Favourable karma from younger people is a great start to the month. Your advice is useful and is based upon solid experience. You may not be paid for your assistance, but will get satisfaction from working for a good cause. Sexual relationships are hot and spicy on the 5th, 6th and 7th. Journeys with a lover are also light-hearted and rejuvenating. Obstacles at work on the 14th? Let others know just where you stand!

Sagittarius
23 November - 21 December

Don't be too clever in the way you communicate. You could be trying to impress others with your know-how, only to find yourself all tangled in knots. Actively listen to what others have to suggest and quietly agree even if you don't. Make your moves after the 18th, when you'll be better informed for an attack. Between the 20th and 22nd, an emotional experience could set you up for a new friendship. Don't play hard to get.

Special
moments

Capricorn
22 December - 20 January

Even if you receive threatening correspondence or harassing phone calls, keep your cool on the 1st. Others will be testing your mettle to see how far they can push you. On the other hand, trouble on the home front will cause you to react excessively, thereby throwing you off-centre and negatively impacting upon your professional responsibilities. Some meditation or the company of calmer people will help you in finding inner peace. Good news on the grapevine can be expected on the 19th.

Aquarius
21 January - 18 February

Your work will find you whizzing here, there and everywhere, especially between the 1st and the 6th. Delegate some responsibility to those who aren't quite as busy. Rumours on the 8th will ruffle your feathers if you read too much into the gossip. Rely on a friend to feed you the correct information before retaliating. A temporary cooling-off of your relationship should be an opportunity for you to re-examine your values this month.

Pisces
19 February - 20 March

Stop interfering in a relative's personal affairs if you want peace of mind. On the 4th, 5th and 6th be a minimalist in your advice and let your actions speak louder than words. A nice relief from antagonistic issues can be expected around the 15th, when you're free to engage in intimate moments with the one you love. An increased social agenda is likely after the 27th.

Word Search

In the Newspaper

```
P  I  E  L  C  I  T  R  A  T  B  R  Y
T  O  T  D  A  I  L  Y  F  Q  P  O  Q
R  Z  O  E  B  S  T  O  R  Y  R  B  V
E  T  G  C  M  W  L  M  N  E  B  I  Z
D  N  R  G  S  W  E  K  P  M  S  T  F
A  E  E  H  P  D  Y  A  P  E  S  U  I
E  T  P  D  I  R  P  C  N  L  E  A  L
R  N  O  A  I  V  I  I  N  Y  R  R  L
F  O  R  V  T  T  L  N  P  E  P  Y  E
O  C  T  P  K  D  O  O  T  K  G  Y  R
O  W  E  I  A  C  C  R  L  E  S  A  Y
R  V  R  E  D  P  W  W  I  P  R  C  N
P  P  H  M  L  E  W  N  R  A  C  Q  M
T  A  B  L  O  I  D  E  C  V  L  X  U
R  C  M  S  I  L  A  N  R  U  O  J  L
P  L  R  V  T  D  Z  T  W  K  K  V  O
K  F  E  N  I  L  D  A  E  D  M  J  C
```

©2006 PuzzleJunction.com

AGENCY	EDITORIAL	PRESS
ARTICLE	FILLER	PRINTER
COLUMN	HEADLINE	PROOFREADER
CONTENT	ITEM	REPORTER
COPY	JOURNALISM	SCOOP
DAILY	MEDIA	SPREAD
DEADLINE	OBITUARY	STORY
EDITOR	PAPER	TABLOID

Special moments

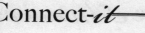

Connect-it

It's Official

Copyright ©2006 PuzzleJunction.com

Each line in the puzzle below has three clues and three
answers. The last letter in the first answer on each line is the
first letter of the second answer, and so on. The connecting
letter is outlined, giving you the correct number of letters for
each answer (the answers in line 1 are 4, 6 and 6 letters).
The clues are numbered 1 to 8, with each number containing
3 clues for the 3 answers on the line. But here's the catch!
The clues are not in order - so the first clue in the line is not
necessarily for the first answer. Good luck!

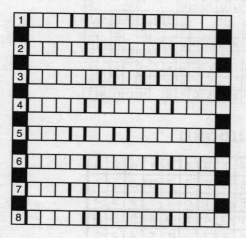

Clues:

1. Branch. Stoat. Church official.
2. Official list or rule. Fault finder. Keepsake.
3. Hardwood. Official seal. Martial art.
4. Official decree. Spirit. King's seat.
5. De-ice. Government official. Toasty.
6. Muffler. Court official. Exit.
7. Mistake. Sports official. At hand.
8. Roosted. Rascal. School official.

387

KRISSKROSS

J	E	T	L	A	G		G	I	V	E	I	N
	A				O		U		O			O
	T	A	K	E	A	I	M		T			W
	O		E		W		U		E			I
	U		E		R		P	A	S	S	O	N
S	T	O	P	B	Y				D			
			U				T	O	O	B	I	G
M	U	D	P	I	E				W			E
E		R			W	H	A	T	N	E	X	T
R		A			E			R		Q		I
R	A	G	D	O	L	L		I		U		N
Y		S			A			E	M	A	I	L
M		O	L	D	M	A	I	D		L		I
E		U			B			O		T		N
N	E	T	L	O	S	S		N	O	O	N	E

SUDOKU

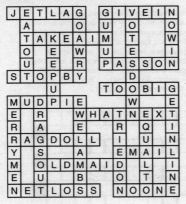

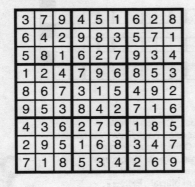

3	7	9	4	5	1	6	2	8
6	4	2	9	8	3	5	7	1
5	8	1	6	2	7	9	3	4
1	2	4	7	9	6	8	5	3
8	6	7	3	1	5	4	9	2
9	5	3	8	4	2	7	1	6
4	3	6	2	7	9	1	8	5
2	9	5	1	6	8	3	4	7
7	1	8	5	3	4	2	6	9

WORDSEARCH

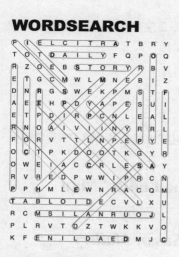

CONNECT-IT

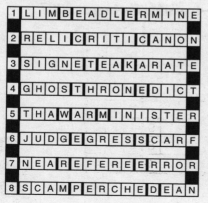

1	L	I	M	B	E	A	D	L	E	R	M	I	N	E
2	R	E	L	I	C	R	I	T	I	C	A	N	O	N
3	S	I	G	N	E	T	E	A	K	A	R	A	T	E
4	G	H	O	S	T	H	R	O	N	E	D	I	C	T
5	T	H	A	W	A	R	M	I	N	I	S	T	E	R
6	J	U	D	G	E	G	R	E	S	S	C	A	R	F
7	N	E	A	R	E	F	E	R	E	E	R	R	O	R
8	S	C	A	M	P	E	R	C	H	E	D	E	A	N

Turn the page for a sneak preview of

The Ladies' Man

by

Susan Mallery

Available in August 2007

The Ladies' Man

by

Susan Mallery

Carter Brockett eyed the curvy brunette in the prim dress and knew he was seconds away from all kinds of trouble. The cool, logical side of his brain reminded him that all the pain and suffering in his life could be traced back to one source: women. Life was always better when he walked away.

The part of his brain—and the rest of him—that enjoyed a warm body, a sharp mind and a purely feminine take on the world said she looked interesting. And that last bit of consciousness, shaped by a very strong-willed mother who had drilled into him that he was always to protect those weaker than him, told him that the attractive brunette was in way over her head.

He could be wrong of course. For all he knew, she was a leather-wearing dominatrix who came to the Blue Dog because of the place's reputation. But he had his doubts.

The Blue Dog was a cop bar. But not just any hangout for those in uniform. It was a place where guys showed up to get lucky and the women who walked in counted on that fact. Carter usually avoided the place— he worked undercover and couldn't afford to be seen here. But one of his contacts had insisted on the location, so Carter had agreed and prayed no one from the force would speak to him.

No one had. He'd concluded his business and had been about to leave when the brunette had walked in with her friend, who was currently involved in a heated conversation with Eddy. Eddy wasn't exactly a prince when it came to his dating habits, so Carter had a feeling the chat wasn't going to go well. He nodded at Jenny, the bartender on duty, then pointed to the brunette. Jenny raised her eyebrows.

Carter didn't have to guess what she was thinking. Jenny, an ex-girlfriend, knew him pretty well. Yeah, well, maybe after a few months of self-induced celibacy, he was ready to give the man-woman thing another try. Even though he knew better. Even though it was always a disaster.

He glanced around and saw he wasn't the only one who'd noticed the contrast between the brunette's made-for-sin body and her Sunday-school-teacher clothes. So if he was going to protect her from the other big bad cops, he'd better get a move on.

He walked to the bar, where Jenny handed him a beer and a margarita. He ignored her knowing grin and crossed to the brunette's table.

"Hi. I'm Carter. Mind if I join you?"

As he asked the question, he set down the margarita and gave her his best smile.

Yeah, yeah, a cheap trick, he thought, remembering all the hours he'd spent perfecting it back in high school. He'd taught himself to smile with just the right amount of interest, charm and bashfulness. It never failed.

Not even tonight, when the woman looked up, flushed, half rose, then sat back down, and in the process knocked over her nearly empty drink and scattered the slushy contents across the table and down the front of her dress.

"Oh, no," she said, her voice soft and almost musical. "Darn. I can't believe I…" She pressed her lips together, then looked at him.

He'd already sopped up the mess on the table with a couple of napkins. He completely ignored the dampness on her dress. Sure, he was interested, but he wasn't stupid.

"You okay?" he asked, curious about a woman who actually said *darn*.

"Yes. Thank you."

He passed over the drink he'd brought.

She glanced first at it, then at him. "I'm, ah, with someone."

He kept his gaze on her. "Your girlfriend. I saw you come in together."

She nodded. "She's breaking up with her boyfriend and wanted moral support. I don't usually… This isn't…" She sighed. "She'll be back soon."

"No problem," he said easily. "I'll keep you company until she's finished."

Even in the dim light of the bar, he could see her eyes were green. Her long, dark hair hung in sensuous waves to just past her shoulders.

Carter held in a snort. Sensuous waves? He'd sure been without for a little too long if he were thinking things like that.

She shifted uncomfortably and didn't touch the drink.

"Is it me or the bar?" he asked.

"What? Oh, both, I suppose." Instantly, she covered her mouth, then dropped her hand to her damp lap. "Sorry. I shouldn't have said that."

"It's fine. I'm a great believer in the truth. So which is more scary?"

She glanced around the Blue Dog, then returned her attention to him. "Mostly you."

He grinned. "I'm flattered."

"Why? You *want* me to think you're scary?"

He leaned forward and lowered his voice just enough to get her to sway toward him. "Not scary. Dangerous. All guys want to be dangerous. Women love that."

She surprised him by laughing. "Okay, Carter, I can see you're a pro and I'm way out of my league with you. I cheerfully confess I'm not the bar type and being in this setting makes me horribly uncomfortable." She glanced at her friend. "I can't tell if the fight's going well or badly. What do you think?"

He looked at Eddy, who'd backed the blonde into a corner. "It depends on how you're defining 'well.' I don't think they're actually breaking up. Do you?"

"I'm not sure. Diane was determined to tell him what she thought, once and for all. In 'I' sentences."

He frowned. "In what?"

She smiled. "*I* think you're not treating me with respect. *I* think you're always late on purpose. That kind of thing. Although she did say something about wanting to kick him in the head, which is unlikely to help. Of course, I don't know Eddy. He may like that sort of thing."

Carter was totally and completely charmed. "Who *are* you?" he asked.

"My name is Rachel."

"You don't swear, you don't hang out in bars, so what do you do?"

"How do you know I don't swear?" she asked.

"You said 'darn' when you spilled your drink."

"Oh. Right. It's a habit. I teach kindergarten. There's no way I can swear in front of the children, not that I ever used a lot of bad words, so I trained myself to never say them. It's just easier. So I use words like 'darn' and 'golly.'" She grinned. "Sometimes people look at me like I'm at the dull-normal end of the IQ scale, but I can live with that. It's for the greater good. So who are you?"

A complicated question, Carter thought, knowing he couldn't tell her the truth. "Just a guy."

"Uh-huh." She eyed his earring—a diamond stud—and his too-long hair. "More than just a guy. What do you do?"

That changed with the assignment, he thought. "I'm working for a chopper shop. Motorcycles," he added.

She straightened her spine and squared her shoulders. "I know what a chopper is. I'm not some innocent fresh out of the backwoods."

Her indignation made him want to chuckle. She reminded him of a kitten facing down a very large and powerful dog. All the arched back and hissing fury didn't make the kitten any bigger.

"Not a lot of backwoods around here," he said easily. "Desert, though. You could be an innocent fresh out of the desert."

Her lips twitched, as if she were trying not to smile. He pushed her margarita toward her.

"You're letting all the ice melt," he told her.

She hesitated, then took a sip. "Are you from around here?" she asked.

"Born and raised. All my family's here."

"Such as?"

Now it was his turn to pause. He didn't usually give out personal information. In his line of work, it could get him into trouble. But he had a feeling Rachel wasn't going to be a threat to much more than his oath of celibacy.

"Three sisters, a mom. Their main purpose in life is

to make me crazy." He made the statement with equal parts love and exasperation.

Rachel looked wistful. "That's nice. Not the crazy part, but that you're close."

"You're not close to your family?"

"I don't have any."

He didn't know what to say to that and reminded himself too late that he was supposed to be charming her, not reminding her that she was alone in the world.

"Are you from around here?" he asked.

"Riverside?" She shook her head. Her hair swayed and caught the light and, for the moment, totally mesmerized him. "I moved here after I graduated from college. I wanted a nice, quiet, suburban sort of place." She sighed. "Not very exciting."

"Hey, I've lived here all my life. I can show you the best spots for viewing the submarine races."

She grinned. "Where I grew up, we went parking over by the river. Well, not really a river. More of a gully. Part of the year, it even had water in it."

"Parking, huh?"

She shrugged. "I had my moments."

"And now?"

Her gaze drifted to where her friend still talked to Eddy. "Not so much." She looked back at him. "Why'd you come over?"

He smiled. "Have you looked in the mirror lately?"

She ducked her head and blushed. Carter couldn't remember the last time he'd seen a woman blush. He wanted to make her do it again.

"Thank you," she said. "I spend my days with five-year-olds whose idea of being charming is to put glue in my hair. You're a nice change."

"You're comparing me to a five-year-old?" he asked, pretending outrage.

"Well, a lot of guys have maturity issues."

"I'm totally mature. Responsible, even."

She didn't look convinced. "Of course you are."

On sale 17th August 2007

WINNING DIXIE
by Janis Reams Hudson

When millionaire Wade Harrison woke from surgery, his first
words were 'Hug my boys.' But he had no boys! Convinced
his heart was telling him to look after his donor's sons, he
headed to Texas...and met their beautiful mother, Dixie
McCormick, who really set his pulse racing!

HIS MOTHER'S WEDDING
by Judy Duarte

PI Rico Garcia's cynicism about marriage put him on a
collision course with gorgeous wedding planner
Molly Townsend. The attraction sizzled...but was it
enough to melt the detective's world-weary veneer?

SUBSTITUTE DADDY
by Kate Welsh

Wealthy playboy Brett Costain and virginal Melissa Abell had
shared a kiss at their siblings' wedding... Now, years later,
a tragedy reunited them, and Brett found that Melissa was
pregnant with the Costain heir. He quickly discovered that he
wanted to be much more than a substitute father...

FREE

4 BOOKS AND A SURPRISE GIFT!

We would like to take this opportunity to thank you for reading this Mills & Boon® book by offering you the chance to take FOUR more specially selected titles from the Special Edition series absolutely FREE! We're also making this offer to introduce you to the benefits of the Mills & Boon® Reader Service™—

> ★ FREE home delivery
> ★ FREE gifts and competitions
> ★ FREE monthly Newsletter
> ★ Books available before they're in the shops
> ★ Exclusive Reader Service offers

Accepting these FREE books and gift places you under no obligation to buy; you may cancel at any time, even after receiving your free shipment. Simply complete your details below and return the entire page to the address below. You don't even need a stamp!

YES! Please send me 4 free Special Edition books and a surprise gift. I understand that unless you hear from me, I will receive 6 superb new titles every month for just £3.10 each, postage and packing free. I am under no obligation to purchase any books and may cancel my subscription at any time. The free books and gift will be mine to keep in any case.

E7ZEE

Ms/Mrs/Miss/Mr..............................Initials ....
BLOCK CAPITALS PLEASE

Surname ....

Address ....

....

....Postcode ....

Send this whole page to:

The Reader Service, FREEPOST CN81, Croydon, CR9 3WZ

Offer valid in UK only and is not available to current Mills & Boon® Reader Service™subscribers to this series. Overseas and Eire please write for details. We reserve the right to refuse an application and applicants must be aged 18 years or over. Only one application per household. Terms and prices subject to change without notice. Offer expires 31st October 2007. As a result of this application, you may receive offers from Harlequin Mills & Boon and other carefully selected companies. If you would prefer not to share in this opportunity please write to The Data Manager at PO Box 676, Richmond, TW9 1WU.

Mills & Boon® is a registered trademark owned by Harlequin Mills & Boon Limited.
The Mills & Boon® Reader Service™ is being used as a trademark.